IN
A
PIG'S
EYE

IN
A
PIG'S
EYE

A Jimmy Flannery Mystery

ROBERT CAMPBELL

POCKET BOOKS

New York London Toronto Sydney Tokyo Singapore

This book is a work of fiction. Names, characters, places and incidents
are either products of the author's imagination or are used fictitiously.
Any resemblance to actual events or locales or persons, living or dead,
is entirely coincidental.

POCKET BOOKS, a division of Simon & Schuster Inc.
1230 Avenue of the Americas, New York, NY 10020

Copyright © 1991 by Robert Campbell

Campbell, Robert.
    In a pig's eye : a Jimmy Flannery mystery / Robert Campbell.
        p.   cm.
    ISBN 0-671-70327-7 : $19.00
    I. Title.
PS3553.A4867 I5 1991
813'.54—dc20   91-21155
                                                                        CIP

First Pocket Books hardcover printing October 1991

10 9 8 7 6 5 4 3 2 1

Printed in the U.S.A.

For George Wager, my old friend, in memory of those times back in the old neighborhood, which was so much like the one in which Jimmy Flannery lives.

1

SOMETIMES I GO OVER TO THE PLAY PARK AND watch the kids playing softball. There's a couple of minutes there, just after the sun goes down but there's still plenty of light in the sky, when things look very sharp and sounds are very clear. The crack of the bat on the softball sounds like the whack of a long fly ball over to Comiskey Park. I watch the ball going up, up, up and I watch the batter racing down to first base, maybe second base, maybe even third, with his hair flying—her hair flying—and there's this look on his face—her face—like the kid'd just won immortality.

And all of a sudden I'm in that kid's body—I don't care if it's a boy or a girl—and I just know for sure that I'm going to be twelve years old forever.

Then that golden instant breaks—pops like a soap bubble—and I ain't a twelve-year-old kid. I'm a grown man who's already lost his mother—God rest her soul—and whose father is retired from the fire department for a few years now, already eligible for Medicare. I'm married to a girl—a woman—by the name of Mary Ellen

Flannery and we're about to have a baby in a couple of weeks now, which naturally means that I'm going to be a father.

I been working in the sewers for a number of years and I been a Democratic Party precinct captain for Committeeman Francis Brendan "Chips" Delvin in the Twenty-seventh Ward for a number of years and I'm very comfortable doing those jobs.

Which ain't to say I don't get promotions. I get promotions. I been promoted to inspector in the sewers and I been asked, more than once, more than twice, to step up in the party. I even passed up a chance to run for alderman, which maybe was just as well because I had a feeling that Janet Canarias, the Puerto Rican lipstick lesbian who whumped the regular Democratic organization's candidate, would've whumped me too. Especially because, if I'd run, my heart wouldn't've been in it. I liked it the way things were. Maybe I wanted to stay twelve years old forever.

But when a man's got a wife and a kid on the way, it means he's got to put aside certain things and accept new responsibilities. Which I done. Which I'm doing.

Like the other Saturday afternoon Delvin calls a meeting of all the precinct captains, which means about twenty-nine people. Men and women. Plus my old man, Mike.

We're gathered over to Brennan's Tavern in the back room where Delvin has his meetings whenever there's too many to fit into his living room. Also Brennan gives him a price on sandwiches and a free first round of drinks which everybody thinks is very nice of him.

We're past the first round and it's now a no-host bar. So all the ones who've had a whiskey or a highball are ordering beers or glasses of white wine which they'll nurse through the rest of the evening unless somebody else springs for a round.

Delvin stands up and clears his throat which is his way of asking for order.

He stands there with his hands flat on the table, his head lowered between his hunched shoulders, looking like some old gorilla, and glares at everybody like he does when he wants to show you how much he loves you.

"So, how many of you figure that I'm going to live forever?"

Everybody's hand, but one, goes up.

"So, you don't think so, Packy?" Delvin says.

"Well, now, Mr. Delvin," Packy Cooley—the one who didn't raise his hand—says, "there's no doubt you'll live for all eternity in the hereafter, but good sense suggests—"

"For Christ's sake, Cooley," Delvin says, beside himself with frustration at the man, "the question was by way of being a little joke. An amusement to break the ice. A proper way to start the proceedings with a little laugh, you understand?"

"Oh, pardon me, pardon me," Cooley says.

Delvin takes the weight off his right hand just long enough to wave Cooley quiet and then he says, "Cooley's let the cat out of the bag. I ain't going to live forever and ain't that a relief?"

Expressions of dismay and protest. "You've got another fifty years at least," Cooley says, making up for lost ground.

"Nah, nah, nah," Delvin says, grinning at their affectionate response. "I've got a few, but you never can tell when that certain somebody's going to tap you on the shoulder."

"Who's that?" Cooley asks belligerently, like he's ready to defend Delvin against all comers.

"The Grim Reaper, you silly sonofabitch. Will you drink your beer, eat your corned beef, open your ears, and shut your mouth, Packy? If you'll stop interrupting, maybe we can be out of here in an hour, maybe less."

Cooley tucks his chin into his chest, indicating his intention of remaining silent from now on.

"It's time for me to lay down some of the burdens I've been carrying these many years," Delvin says. "It's time for new blood in the party, especially now that Hizzoner—God rest his soul—Richard J. Daley's kid, is sitting in the mayor's office. It's time for the regular organization to be a power in Chicago once again and we need young men to lead us."

Everybody under forty in the room starts looking this way, that way, to see if other people got their eyes on him or her which could mean that they've been tipped about who Delvin's nominee to take his place as warlord of the Twenty-seventh is going to be.

I don't look around because Delvin's already told me a hundred times that I'm going to be the man and he's invited my father, which he wouldn't do if he intended to humiliate me. However, in case he's changed his mind—which he's been known to do—and he ends up naming somebody else—which is always a possibility— I don't want anybody to be looking at my face when Delvin gives us the news.

"There's one of you that's always been right out there doing the job, registering the voters, serving the people in his precinct, getting out the vote on election day. Even turning a couple of Republicans around from time to time. I ain't saying he's the only one who's worked hard . . ."

So, okay, right there he said *he* which means the ladies are not in the running.

". . . there's plenty of you who've worked hard. But the candidate I got in mind has always put out a little extra. Sometimes he's put out a little extra where maybe he shouldn't've put out a little extra, but that's

4

okay, too, if you don't carry it too far. Also I got to admit . . ."

A little extra could mean Dinny Kiernan's work with the Boy's Athletic Club or Billy Scanlan's activities in the Knights of Columbus or Charlie Bill's run, without benefit of the party's sanction, for the state legislature a couple of years ago or even Jack Maggioni's volunteer work over to the Illinois Eye and Ear Infirmary. So now I got it whittled down to me and four others.

". . . this person I got in mind has done me a personal favor from time to time, not because I was the committeeman or the alderman—when I was the alderman—but out of friendship, pure and simple."

Which could be practically anybody in the room because Delvin has a way of getting people to do personal favors for him, but I don't know of any special favors Kiernan, Scanlan, Bill, or Maggioni's done for him lately and I just kept his picture out of the papers not long ago.

Anyway he's got his eye on me, enjoying the little torture he's putting me through. Knowing how my mind works. How I'd be sitting there taking clues from what he's saying, figuring out step by step who it was he was about to hand the crown to. Letting me twist and turn in the breeze a little bit before cutting me down.

"Without further ado, in these few moments before I ask you to vote for the next committeeman of the Twenty-seventh Ward from among yourselves—understanding that I am not exerting any undue pressure in this democratic proceeding—I would like to offer the name of James Flannery for your consideration."

There's some applause and a lot of smiles on the faces turned to me. Mike grins from ear to ear and grabs my arm with his big hand, which reminds me of the time I won a prize for baseball when I was in high school.

It's electric when your father does something like that when you've done something good.

But it's also this part of doing something grand or doing somebody a favor or getting a promotion that makes me feel uncomfortable. All the grinning and clapping and the eyes on you.

I get uncomfortable when somebody thanks me for doing them a favor. I mean if I can do something to help a person, why shouldn't I do it? The way I figure, you help somebody else, you help yourself, because it's always better to spread a little cheer instead of a little gloom. It's always better to give somebody a helping hand than to walk on by. You never know when you're going to need a hand, and if everybody gets into the habit of taking care of number one and the hell with everybody else, there's not going to be very many hands reaching out to save you when you start going under for the third time.

"Any other nominations?" Delvin asks.

A couple of hands go up. Millie Jefferson, who's been wanting a black committeeman or woman for years, raises her hand. Helen Reeba, who wants the same for the Hispanics, raises hers. Dan McGuire—who's never been very friendly to me ever since I made it look like I was going to let Baby, the gorilla, get to his friend Big Buck Baily over to the zoo—sticks up his paw. Also, Packy Cooley clears his throat and gets to his feet.

Delvin looks a little surprised.

Now the way it works, when and if a ward committeeman steps down, and unless the president of the Cook County Democratic Central Committee or the mayor or some other party boss has somebody for the job, then the retiring committeeman makes his or her choice for his or her successor and the precinct captains toe the line and that's that.

However, any captain can offer a candidate and it's

even happened that a retiring warlord ain't been too popular, or the man or woman he chooses to take his place has made a lot of enemies, and the committeeman don't get his way. His pick loses the election. This could maybe be one of those times the warlord's pick don't get the crown. Not because Delvin's unpopular or even that I'm unpopular but because times are changing and the old ways are dying out.

"What is it, Packy?" Delvin asks, with this attitude that says he's being very patient with Cooley but it ain't easy, when all the time I know and maybe everybody else knows that Cooley and Delvin were boyhood chums and Cooley would never do anything to really harm or thwart Delvin but just liked to get his goat now and then.

Cooley clears his throat again and takes a swallow of his beer.

"Is this going to take awhile?" Delvin asks.

"Committeeman Delvin," Cooley says. "Chips. I'd like to enter into nomination for the position of committeeman of the Twenty-seventh Democratic Ward of the great city of Chicago, one Francis Brendan Delvin."

There's a burst of applause because here's Cooley paying the old man this great tribute. Jefferson and Reeba have their hands occupied clapping but they're working out the consequences, now that Cooley's handed the palm back to Delvin, if they toss somebody else's hat in the ring.

"Wait a second, wait a second," Delvin protests, pleased as Punch. "I ain't running for the office. I'm giving it up. You understand what I'm saying? I can't be a candidate."

"But that don't mean I can't put your name into nomination," Cooley says. "After we vote you back into office, you don't want the job, all you got to do is appoint somebody to serve out your term and then resign."

Well, that's not the way it's supposed to work, and everybody knows it. But anything less than going along is going to be a big insult to the old man. Jefferson and Reeba glance over at me and smile.

They know and I know that Cooley's snookered them and pulled their claws before they could give me and Delvin even a little scratch.

"Call the vote! Call the vote!" Cooley yells out.

"Show of hands! Show of hands!" somebody else shouts.

"All those in favor of James Flannery?" Cooley says, taking over the chair without protest.

Not a hand goes up.

"All those in favor of Francis Delvin."

Every hand goes up.

Delvin gets up on his feet, wipes a tear from his eye, gives Jefferson and Reeba one of his sweetest smiles, and glances over at Dan McGuire, who's sitting there glowering. Delvin, knowing he's been snookered, too, gives Cooley half a wink, thanks everybody and turns the chair and the job over to me to another round of spontaneous applause.

I'm the warlord, the committeeman of the Twenty-seventh, the ward leader. I ain't twelve years old any more.

It's time for me to make a little thank you speech, which I do, keeping it short and sweet, and then I call for drinks all around on me, which everybody thinks is a grand way for me to start my term of office. I don't even drink but the tab comes to a small bundle what with everybody switching from beer and wine to boiler-makers and fancy cocktails.

2

MARY'S VERY HAPPY TO HEAR ABOUT THE honor that's been handed me, even given the fact that Jefferson and a couple of others wanted to put up people to run against me. To be very honest I think it was more by way of pushing forward their personal agendas than to mount any serious challenge to me becoming ward leader. I mean I think I would've got the job no matter what, even though I'm still not so sure I really want it.

It could mean two things. One, I probably won't see as much of my own people—my friends and neighbors—from my own precinct, and two, I'm going to have to find a place where the people in the ward can come to me at least once a week and make their complaints and ask the favors that the precinct captains can't manage on their own. Also, the captains will be coming to this place once a week to give me a report on how things are going in their precincts, people moving in, moving out, coming of voting age, and passing away. In other words, instead of me walking around saying hello and asking what I can do to help, I'll be waiting for them to come to me simply because a ward's too big for me to get to know that well on foot. I'll be like a cop who used to walk a foot patrol and knew everybody on his beat but now has to ride in a car through fifty times as many streets and don't know scarcely a soul.

We'd already agreed not to make any special fuss about it at home. It was only supposed to be Mary and me; my father; her mother, Charlotte, and her Aunt Sada; my dog, Alfie; and the tenants who are part owners with Mary and me in the apartment building.

But when I get home there are all kinds of people lining the stairway and gathered on the landing in front of our flat on the third floor. Pearl and Joe Pakula, what own the grocery store downstairs on the corner; Janet Canarias, the alderwoman; Willy Dink, the exterminator; Shimmy Dugan and Princess Grace who own a bathhouse called the Paradise which they turned into a health club called the same over on Warren and Damen near the Chicago Stadium; Bo Addison, this junk artist; and God knows how many others, a couple of whom I don't even think I know. Strangers who probably saw the crowd and figured there was a chance to see a celebrity or maybe get in on a free feed or something.

I had two or three corned beef sandwiches and three or four soda pops over to Brennan's, so the going up the stairs, with everybody patting me and hugging me and kissing me on the cheeks, takes the breath out of me.

In the dining room, the table's set with a nice spread of cold cuts, bread, and salads, plus beverages on ice. There's casseroles and hot dishes in the kitchen.

I can't resist. I have a little taste of everything and a couple bottles of orange soda.

Mary comes over and gives me a kiss on the side of the mouth.

"You're shooting your diet to hell," she whispers.

"Well, I don't know how it would've looked over to

Brennan's if I refused Delvin's hospitality. Also it wouldn't look right if I don't take a little something to eat in my own home at my own party in my own honor, which I thought we agreed you weren't going to make such a big thing over because you could have the baby any minute now."

"Not any minute or any hour. Not even any day now. A few weeks yet. We had to do a little something. Your constituents wanted to congratulate you and celebrate with you."

"They ain't exactly my constituents since I wasn't elected to public office or anything like that."

"So, whatever you want to call it," she said. "I just want to mention that this party doesn't give you an excuse."

"An excuse for what?"

"Missing your exercise class."

Maybe I should mention that ever since Mary told me she was pregnant, I've been eating more than I usually do. Nervousness is what it is. Also something's happening to my metabolism. I look at a grape, I put on a pound.

Mary's watching her own weight like a hawk, eating just right for herself and the baby. Which means I get to eat the same at home. Lots of salads and things like that. But she knows I don't eat the same when I'm outside.

It's very hard for a man raised on meat and potatoes to do entirely without a hamburger or a steak and fries now and then.

Well, anyway, I signed up for these classes at the Paradise. I been going three times a week. Tuesday, Thursday, and Saturday nights.

So there I am having to excuse myself from my own party to go over to the Paradise Health Club with

Shimmy Dugan and Princess Grace and get into a sweat suit with a bunch of other baby porkers and go bouncing around, with Princess Grace—all rigged out in shiny pink tights and a powder blue chiffon scarf around his neck—yelling instructions and counting cadence until I'm about to drop.

Princess Grace is a black man of the gay persuasion which don't mean he ain't as tough as a Marine drill instructor when it comes to making you do the knee bends and duck waddles.

I can imagine everybody back at my flat scarfing up the corned beef and potato salad while I'm listening to "Down and up and right side, left side. And down and up and right side, left side annnnnnd rest."

It's enough to make a strong man weep.

All this fat bouncing up and down and rolling around the floor, it's a wonder we don't all go busting through into the basement.

Which is not to say that everybody's a porker in the group. There's a couple of men what are body builders and do the aerobics for endurance and a few young women who are built very nicely indeed and only *think* they need to lose some pounds.

One of them, a girl by the name of Lucy Frye, is in the row in front of me, just to the right of this heavyweight buster who's going at it like he wants to lose a hundred by nightfall.

On the other side of him is a Mrs. Falzone who makes two of Lucy Frye. Mrs. Falzone and the heavyweight buster look like a couple of those hippopotamuses what was in that Disney picture years ago and which they rerelease every once in a while.

Since that's my choice of views, you can understand that I spend most of my time looking at Lucy Frye jumping up and down, which is a pretty sight.

I don't know the name of the guy in front of me. I

seen him at the health club several times in the last few weeks—we even said hello—but I don't know his name. Either he never told me or I forgot. All I know is that he seems to take the exercise very seriously and smiles a lot.

I remember thinking the first time I met him that he came from Mediterranean stock like Sicilian, southern Italian, or Greek. Either that or he had a very nice tan for a person living in Chicago. The only thing was, for a man with such an olive complexion, he had very blue eyes which you don't often see on somebody from that neck of the woods.

Anyway, after a little standing and heavy breathing, we get down on the floor again and start another exercise that includes a lot of leg lifting and torso raising which knocks everybody out pretty good, except for a couple of the body builders and Princess Grace who's turning into a regular Iron-Man woman or vice versa.

When the exercise ends, we all just lay there resting and then Princess Grace tells us to get up and get ready for the next set.

The skinny ones pop up like a bunch of kangaroos. The rest of us roll over and make it to our knees or scramble onto our feet one way or another like a bunch of turtles knocked on our backs and left high and dry on some beach.

Except for the man who smiles all the time. He ain't smiling now. He's just laying there on his back with his palms flat on the floor like a beached baby whale. His mouth is open and his eyes are half closed.

"Up, up, up, Mr. . . . uh . . ." Princess Grace says, skipping over, a little frown on his face because he don't remember the man's name either.

The baby whale don't make a move.

I walk over as Princess Grace sticks out the toe of his

ballet slipper and gives the man a playful little poke in the side. Still no response.

I go down on one knee and look into what I can see of his eyes. The half-circle of the iris of each one has a narrow line of milky blue-white around it. I can tell just by looking that the man's gone, but I put my fingers on the artery in the neck anyways, just to be sure. Also it looks like I know what I'm doing, which I think a ward leader should try to do.

I look up at Princess Grace. "If I was you, I'd clear the room, Princess, because this man's dead."

3

WHEN ANYBODY DIES SUDDEN LIKE THAT, THE first thing you think of is heart attack. I mean the time that Shecky Albinato keeled over face down into the minestrone over to the Thirty-sixth Ward's annual fund raiser back in '88, it was heart that took him. When Ryan Quaid died doing the old two-step in Boom-Boom Sullivan's flat over to the Back of the Yards, it was heart. When the priest, who was partying incognito, succumbed in the arms of Shirley Mulligan in Molly Danaher's upstairs bedroom over to the First, some said it was the good Lord punishing him for his transgressions, but Dr. Mayer said it was heart.

Men of a certain age and certain habits got these time bombs ticking away in their chests. If it wasn't the wrong time, I would've got right down there and done another twenty pushups or duck waddles, this man dying like that on the floor scared me so bad.

"I don't know why everything happens to me," Princess Grace says.

"What do you mean?" I says. "It looks to me that

what happened just now didn't happen to you, it happened to this man laying on the floor."

"Well, I mean first it's gorillas spending the night in the steam room and giving the place a bad name and now it's somebody kicking off while doing the exercises that was supposed to make him healthy. I mean things like that are kicking the hell out of the credibility of my establishment. You sure he's dead?"

"See for yourself."

Princess Grace pulls his hands up like a puppy begging and says as how he'd rather not. "Don't you think we ought to get him up off the floor?" he adds. "He looks so uncomfortable there."

I don't see how that would do any harm. After all, the man ain't been shot or stabbed. It ain't a crime scene where you have to tell everybody not to touch anything.

"I don't see why not," I says. "Where you want him put?"

"In the men's locker room? You could put him on one of the benches."

"I don't think that'd be too good. People got to get dressed and undressed in there."

"How about the steam room?"

"Well, for God's sake, Princess, some of the people here might like a little steam and I don't think it would do this gentleman much good. All that heat and humidity."

I can tell he don't want to do it, but finally Princess Grace agrees to having the body carried to his office— which he was at pains to say he'd just had redecorated— and put down on the couch in there.

I get the two men body builders and another guy to take a corner and I'm about to take one for myself when this big blonde woman, about thirty-five, five foot eleven, a hundred and sixty pounds, nudges me aside and says she's ready to lend a hand.

Her name's Marcie O'Leary and she's always looking for a chance to prove that women can do anything men can do and a couple of things they can't.

So I says okay, heave-ho, and they pick up our friend and haul him off to the office where Princess Grace's partner and significant other, Shimmy Dugan, is working on the books.

He looks up in surprise when I knock on the glass window in the door, then walk on in lugging a corpse with the three men and a girl in leotards and sweats.

"Somebody have a little faint?" he says, getting up from his desk.

"Somebody had a little something more serious than a faint."

"A swoon?"

"A knockout. A fatal. A swan."

"Well, put him down on the couch, then, and can you take off his shoes? That cover's brand new."

After they lay him down, I fold the poor man's hands on his chest and take off his shoes, which are brand new running types that go out at a hundred forty bucks a copy retail.

Marcie leaves with the other three body builders which leaves me alone with Dugan, Princess Grace, and the dead man.

"You know who this is?" I asks.

Dugan puts a finger on his lip like he's thinking it over, and when he can't come up with a name, goes to the books. He looks them over for quite awhile, checking the day of the week against the membership list, comparing this one here with that one there, trying to figure out by a process of elimination who this guy can be.

"That's funny," he says, "I don't think I've got a name on this client."

"How's that?"

"Well, I remember now the day he came in and took

out a trial membership. When I asked him his name, he patted his stomach and made a kind of self-deprecatory remark about Porky Pig. You know, like that cartoon character?"

I said I knew.

"After we had our little laugh, I suppose he just walked on out without me getting his real name, so I just put down P. Pig, figuring I'd get his real name on the books another time."

"Couldn't you get his name off his check?"

"He paid in cash."

"How much was the trial membership?"

"Twenty dollars."

"And how long was it good for?"

"Two weeks. Didn't you take out a trial?"

"No, I took a regular."

He glances down at his books.

"I got you down for twenty bucks."

"You made me a price."

"Oh. Well, okay, I made you a price. How come I made you a price?"

"You wanted me to look into getting you a beer and wine license."

"What have you got to do with beer and wine licenses?"

"Nothing. I told you that. But you said maybe I could have a word with the ward committeeman, with Chips Delvin."

"Hey, you're the committeeman now."

"That's right. I was elected to the position this afternoon. You was there at the celebration at my flat a couple of hours ago."

"So now you can do us something about a beer and wine license."

"What for do you need a beer and wine license in a health club?"

"Well, you know, wine and beer are foods. You understand that?"

"That may be, but it still looks very strange a health club asking for a beer and wine license."

"But you'll look into it for us, see what you can do?"

"I'll see what I can do. Now about this person laying on your couch with the new cover. I'm pretty sure I seen him around here more than two weeks."

"Oh, yes," Princess Grace says. "He's been with us a lot longer than that."

"So what kind of membership did he take out after the trial membership?"

Dugan checks his records once more. "He went week to week."

"Ain't it a lot more expensive that way?"

"I remember now. He said he wanted a week-to-week because he didn't know how long he'd be around the neighborhood. He said he never knew when he'd be called away, so he wanted to go week to week."

"And paid you in cash."

"That's right."

"You got a picture of him?"

"Picture?"

"You know, like the picture you took of me for the before and after so your customers—"

"Clients," Princess Grace says.

"—can check their progress."

Dugan goes back to the file and comes up with a file folder. He takes out two prints of a four by five photo of P. Pig. He's standing there in his shorts, this big blubbery man, with knock-knees and a huge grin on his face. For a minute there I can't figure out who he reminds me of, and then it hits me. The way he's standing, the big grin, the look of innocent pleasure on his face, is exactly like a picture my old man's got of me when I was a fat little kid of maybe four or five. That's what

19

P. Pig looked like—a fat little kid having fun and feeling proud of hisself.

"Can I have one of these?" I asks.

"What do you want it for?"

"Family joke. I want to show it to my father."

"Go ahead, take it," Dugan says.

"So maybe we better call the paramedics and the cops and tell them we got a fatality at the Paradise," I says.

"And while we're waiting, we can take a peek in his pockets and find out who he is, for heaven's sake," Princess Grace says. "Curiosity's killing me."

Since there's no suspicion of mayhem here, I don't see any reason why not, though there's no pockets in Porky's shorts and sweat shirt to look through.

Princess checks Porky's locker assignment while Dugan calls 911.

Then we go into the men's locker room to see what we can find in his street clothes. Of course, he's got a combination lock on his locker.

"Well, I guess that settles that," I says.

"Settles what?" Princess Grace says. "We've got to get his clothes for when they take him away. He can't travel in his shorts and sweat shirt."

"What are you talking about?" Dugan says. "They're not going to dress the body in street clothes just to take him down to the morgue and undress him for the autopsy."

"Autopsy?" Princess Grace chirps.

"Certainly. A person dies suddenly when not under a doctor's care, there's got to be an autopsy."

"So, how do we know he's not under a doctor's care? And how are we going to know if he's under a doctor's care if we don't look through his things and see if he's got a prescription or an appointment card or even a physician's name? Something like that?"

"The Princess has a point there," Dugan says.

The lock's one of those cheap combinations you can buy in any five and dime. One tap with a hammer will usually pop the shank loose.

When I ask them if they happen to have a hammer handy, Princess Grace makes a fist and punches the lock with the side of his hand, popping it open.

I'm amazed. "How did you do that? I mean I didn't know you was that strong."

"Don't let the lisp fool you," Princess Grace says in a voice an octave lower and a grade rougher than the breathy voice he usually uses, revealing the tough street kid underneath the flit and flutter.

He removes the lock and opens the locker.

We take out a two piece gray summer-weight suit on a wire hanger, a blue and white striped shirt, a solid maroon tie, and a pair of black and white wing tips with a pair of gray socks rolled up and stuffed into one of them. Also a cheap Leatherette briefcase.

For a minute we hesitate about going into the man's pockets, like we did about breaking into his locker, but then we give each other the nod. Dugan and Princess Grace step back to let me know they expect me to do the honors.

"Well, we should at least find out if this poor man's got a name," I says, and start doing the job.

He's got a fifty-nine cent hard rubber comb in the right back pocket of his pants and a wallet in the left one. There's a used handkerchief—a bandana like a farmer might carry—in his left side pocket and a fold of money in a large ordinary paper clip. Plus there's some change in the right.

Dugan counts the money while I peek into the wallet. No driver's license, no credit cards, no membership cards to clubs or credit unions, no bank identification cards. No more money. Nothing but a piece of note paper about four inches square, folded once, with some handwriting on both sides.

"Fifty-two dollars in bills," Dugan says. "A dollar and twenty-nine cents in change. American."

"American?" I says, wondering why he'd say that.

He holds out his hand. There's several silver coins in his palm, maybe five or six.

"Lire," Dugan says. "Italian lire."

"Thirty lire," Princess Grace says, adding them up.

I pick one up to get a better look.

"Thirty pieces of silver?" I says.

"Jesus Christ," Princess Grace says, not liking it at all, him being very much into all kinds of Central American mumbo jumbo lately.

"God, I hope it's nothing like that," I says.

Dugan lays the lire down on the bench with the other stuff. I look them over and check the dates, all back before I was born. A 1914, two 1930s, and two 1927s, one of which I got in may hand when Princess Grace asks me, "What's it say?" pointing to the slip of paper I'm also holding.

" 'Tenants 5A!' " it says, with an exclamation mark right after it, just like that, the pencil pressed down so hard it makes a scar on the paper. " 'We have lived in this building for three years and have had no quarrel with anyone, but the situation up above us in your apartment has become unbearable to the people who have to live below you . . . which is us.

" 'We have spent many sleepless nights while you run through your apartment and move your furniture and other objects around.

" 'Also, when you flush your toilet, it makes a terrible noise in our apartment. At times you seem to use it seven or eight times in a row. I'm sure you are also annoyed with the sound of the flush. Can't you get the landlord to fix it? Are you not well? Can't you see a doctor?

" 'I am sure that you are not creating these annoyances intentionally, for spite or anything like that, since we don't even know you. We have had words one time and we hardly ever even lay eyes on you.

" 'I am writing this at 1 A.M. in the morning after you woke up both my wife and me from a sound sleep with your tramping around, rearranging furniture, and flushing the toilet.

" 'This has been going on for some time and it is in desperation that I am writing you.

" 'I would suggest that you use bedroom slippers late at night. Also that you complain to the landlord about the flush. Also that you should see a doctor if you are not feeling well.

" 'Please do not think that I am trying to run your private life. I am just annoyed and past the point of desperation.' "

"Is it signed?" Dugan asks.

" 'Mr. Amico in Apartment 4A.' "

"What's going on here?" this voice growls.

It's O'Shea and Rourke, these two homicide dicks from the Monroe District, the Twelfth station house. The one what growled is O'Shea who always looks like he's got a bad case of indigestion and plays the bad cop. Rourke, who's got a very sweet face and disposition, plays the good cop but between the two, if I had to face it out or duke it out, I'd rather go up against O'Shea than Rourke any day of the week. There's something about the rage of a very quiet, easy-going man that can be very intimidating.

"Up to your usual tricks, are you, Flannery?" O'Shea goes on. "Picking pockets, doing a little thievery?"

I hand Rourke the note and stick my other hand with the lire in it into my pocket.

Rourke grins and shakes his head like he's amused by a couple of pals who like to take the mickey out of one another, though he should know by now that O'Shea and me ain't buddies.

"What are you doing here?" I asks.

"You got a dead body, ain't you?"

"We got a man what keeled over with a heart attack, is what we got. All we called for was an ambulance, not an investigation."

"So, you're a doctor now, are you?" O'Shea says.

I look at Rourke, hoping to get a straight answer.

"Could you believe it, we got a slow day for once. Captain Pescaro sees us with our feet up for five minutes and has a fit. Asks us if that's all we got to do when your call come in. Next thing you know he tells us to come have a look, a thing like this. So, we'll have a look, keep Pescaro sweet."

"What've you got in your hand?" O'Shea asks.

"A note I took from the man's pocket."

"What are you doing going through his pockets? First you're a doctor, now you're a coroner?"

"What are you making a case out of here?" I says. "The man dies while he's exercising. Princess Grace and Shimmy Dugan here, the proprietors of this establishment—"

"I know who is Princess Grace and Shimmy Dugan."

"—naturally want to know who the man is so they can send a note of condolence or whatever to the wife or whoever after the police have informed the relatives or whenever."

"They don't know who he is? The man comes here, jumps around in shorts and a sweat shirt, and they don't know the man's name?"

"An oversight," Dugan says. "One of those little administrative details that slip through the cracks."

O'Shea glares at him as though that's suspicious

enough to call for thumb screws and twelve smacks with a wet towel.

"Can I see that?" Rourke says very pleasantly, and I hand over the two pieces of paper.

"What else you find in the poor bastard's pockets?" O'Shea demands.

He holds out his hands and Dugan fills them with the money, the comb, and the used handkerchief, and I top the pile with the empty wallet.

"There's some Italian money there," I says.

"Italian money?" O'Shea says. "What would anybody be doing carrying around Italian money? There any place a person can spend Italian money in Chicago?"

"He could've just got back from a trip to Italy," Princess Grace says.

"Or somebody could've put it in his pocket."

"Like who?"

"Like I don't know."

"You check the pockets in his suit coat?" Rourke asks.

"No."

"All right, then, let's do that."

"The bunch of you can get the hell out of here," O'Shea says.

Princess Grace pulls hisself up and strikes a pose, ready to tell O'Shea to go to hell or shove it or something, but Rourke's right there again, keeping the water smooth.

"What difference does it make, Frank? Let them have a look. Maybe they can tell us something helpful."

"Like what?" O'Shea asks.

"Like I don't know, Frank, but it won't hurt to find out."

4

WHILE THE REST OF US WATCH, ROURKE GOES through the man's coat pockets. In the one on the right hand side there's a roll of Life Saver candies—Wint-O-Green—and the left one's empty. There's nothing in the handkerchief pocket. The right hand breast pocket's also empty but Rourke pulls something out of the left hand one.

He fans out some photographs, then lays them out on a bench like he's dealing out a hand of cards.

I take a look and get the same funny, kind of melancholy, feeling I always get when I look at old photos.

The first one is of a man standing in front of a painted backdrop with three skinny little greyhounds at his feet. The man's leaning on a walking stick and has a short whip in his other hand. He looks a little bit like that French painter with the short legs—what with the beard and the kind of glasses what stay on because they're pinching his nose—who painted all them cancan dancers, except he's got regular legs and even looks like he was pretty tall. On the bottom is printed "Giovanni Guisti, Fotografo, Napoli, Via Cortina 30."

The second photo is on thinner paper. The same man is standing in the middle of some ferns and reeds at the edge of a grove of trees. He's wearing a straw hat and he's also leaning on a walking stick.

The third one is of a young woman with a nice figure, standing at the end of a little dock by a lake. Her face is in the shadow cast by this big hat she's wearing, but you can still see she's very pretty.

The fourth and last photo is of the dog-lover in the beard standing in a garden with the young woman, with the statue of a Greek lady on pedestal just behind them over to the right.

There's no printing or writing on the front of any of the last three pictures and no printing or writing on the backs of any of them except the one of the man in the straw hat by the woods. It was made up into a postcard like they used to do.

"So, that wasn't much. Let's see what we got in here," O'Shea says and unzips the Leatherette briefcase.

He takes out a handful of girlie magazines. Not the *Penthouse* and *Playboy* variety. These got titles like *Torrid Zones* and *Hot Nites*.

I pick one up and leaf through it. There's a bunch of not very good black and whites of some women what the movies and television call bimbos. They're not outstandingly good-looking but some of them is well endowed. One color double-spread of the only really pretty girl in the magazine is in the middle. The staples are in the most unfortunate spots on her anatomy.

She's dark-haired and what they call doe-eyed. Nothing hard about her, though the corners of her mouth look a little tight as though she's seen more than a girl with an innocent face like hers should've seen.

"Getting your kicks, Flannery?" O'Shea says in a nasty way.

I toss the magazine back on the pile.

"You sure one of you ain't pocketed something?" O'Shea says, turning his attention to Princess Grace.

"You thinking of doing a body search, you better warm your hands first, darling," Princess Grace says in his flutiest voice.

"Ah, fachrissake," O'Shea says.

"You go around talking about body searches, you better have reasonable cause," Dugan says. "Otherwise you could have an unlawful search charge on your hands."

"And seizeure," Princess Grace says. "Unlawful search and *seize*-ure."

Rourke laughs and O'Shea turns red.

"Well, Flannery?" he says to me.

I'm very aware of the fact that I got that lire piece in my pocket but it's too late to hand it over after O'Shea accusing me of stealing from a dead man.

"Well, what, O'Shea? If you want to search me, go ahead, but first it'd be nice if you'd tell me what the hell reason I'd have to lift the identity off somebody I was never even introduced to. All I ever saw of this poor guy was his backside jumping up and down and rolling around the floor. Besides which, if I was a thief, why didn't I pocket the cash?"

"Because you heard us coming."

"So, if I heard you coming and couldn't steal the money, when did I have the chance to steal anything else?"

"You could've—"

"Oh, for God's sake, Frank, give it a rest," Rourke says. "The next thing you know you'll be accusing Jimmy here of murdering the man."

From the look on O'Shea's face I could see that he considered that something devoutly to be wished.

5

I ALREADY ANNOUNCED THAT I'D BE AVAILABLE
to the precinct captains over to Brennan's in the back
room on Saturday afternoons if they wanted a meeting,
letting them know that I intend to keep a lot of the old
venues and traditions.

But I also decide that Monday nights, which was
going to be my night to take care of any complaints or
requests my precinct captains didn't think they could
handle, is going to be held somewhere different.

I mention this Sunday night at supper. There's me and
my old man and Mary and Janet Canarias, who stops by
practically every evening to see how Mary's doing and,
a lot of times, stays to help make supper and sit down
with us.

When supper's over, Mike and Mary go into the living
room to watch a little television because I said they
should.

Janet and me are doing the dishes, me washing and
her drying.

She congratulates me again for being the new Democratic Committeeman of the Twenty-seventh and says, "You said you were looking for a place to meet the people and I don't know if it would be the smartest thing in the world to ask the blacks and Hispanics— which, in case you didn't notice, you've got more of in your ward than anybody else—to walk into the back room of another white tavern like Brennan's to ask favors from an Anglo."

"Thanks very much for the advice," I says, "but anybody with eyes in their head can see that."

"I didn't mean to offend you, Jimmy," she says. "I just wanted to remind you because you've lived in your neighborhood all your life and your neighborhood's in a mainly white precinct in a mainly black ward."

"I'm not taking offense, Janet. I appreciate you're taking the time to talk to me about what I got to watch out for with this new job. I'm just saying I know the Twenty-seventh was one of the old plantation wards from way back, with blacks living in it and even representing it sometimes, but whites like Chips Delvin, who lived in other neighborhoods, running it," I says.

"Chips Delvin," she says, like she don't want to say any more about what she thinks about him for my sake.

"Oh, I know the papers call him a 'sewer boss' and claim he runs the department and hands out thousands of patronage jobs—before the courts put the kibosh on most of that—without knowing anything about sewers except how to lift a manhole cover and see if everything's moving along, but I got to tell you, Janet, there's a lot of people, black and white and in between, who think the world of him."

"I won't argue the point," she says. "Now that he's handed over the ward to you, do you think he'll be handing over the sewer department, too?"

"He hasn't got that kind of power any more. Maybe he never did," I says.

"Even so, his recommendation might count for something."

"It might."

"What is it, Jimmy?"

Three, maybe four, people in my life could read me like a book. My mother—God rest her soul—my wife Mary, and Janet Canarias, who started out being kind of a political pain in the neck but ended up being Mary's best friend and a very good friend to me. Also my old man, Mike Flannery, who can almost always tell when things ain't sitting right with me. But it's the women who seem to know something's troubling me almost before I know that something's troubling me. Also, sometimes, Mary's mother Charlotte.

"Something's bothering you," she says.

"I don't know if I want to be the head of the sewer department," I says. "I ain't got the knowledge. I ain't got the education."

"You've walked every foot of those sewers."

That makes me smile though it ain't really very funny walking them miles of scary pipes. "Well, I got to admit I done that," I says.

"It's mostly meetings and paper work," she says. "You've got all sorts of engineers and specialists and superintendents actually running it for you. Your job would be mostly dealing with people and you've got to admit yourself, you're very good at that."

"I guess I am, but shoving paper around and sitting on my duff listening to people yammer about ways and means, instead of getting out there and doing what's got to get done, could turn me into a stone. I'm used to being out on the streets, moving around, going here and there, up and down, you know what I mean?"

"Well, yes, here and there, up and down," she says. "I can understand that."

She's talking to me very seriously, but there's this

little smile tugging at the corners of her mouth, which I understand. People try to talk serious about sewers and sewerage and serious matters like that, but they can't help it, they think there's something funny about it. I can understand that, even though they wouldn't think it was so funny if their toilets didn't flush or if the system backed up into their living room.

"Anyway, that's not something I got to think about at the minute," I says. "What I got to think about is getting a place where the people can come talk to me if they want to."

"When are you going to have your weekly open house?" she asks.

"Well, I thought Mondays."

"That's right. You mentioned Mondays at supper."

"Mondays wouldn't be good?"

"No, I think it would be good. It would be good for me."

"For you?"

"It would be good for me if you wanted to use my storefront on Mondays. I don't have my open house on Mondays."

This storefront on Gaylord Street, about four blocks from where we're standing at the sink doing the dishes, is the storefront which her supporters rented for her—at a very good price—during her successful campaign for alderman. She decided to hold onto it because she wanted a place where people could come see her who might be nervous or reluctant about seeing her in her office down to City Hall. She pays the rent out of her own pocket.

She sees me hesitating and says, "Are you worried that people will think you've bolted the party and gone independent?"

"No, I can find a way to make it clear where I stand.

I'm just wondering if you're going to want me doing favors for people who are also your people."

"What do you mean?"

"Well, I open my doors—which are also your doors—to do favors for everybody who needs a favor, I'm going to make the point that it's the regular organization of the Democratic Party that's giving them a helping hand."

"But you don't ask them for a promise to vote for your candidates?"

"I don't ask—I never asked and I don't ask—but it's the understanding."

"Well, I beat the candidate the regular organization put up against me before," she says, "so that doesn't worry me much. I think we're both after the same thing, Jimmy, doing what we can for people who need help."

"I wouldn't argue with that."

"So, will you accept my offer?"

"Only if we can agree on what rent I'm going to pay you."

"It's sitting there dark Monday nights."

"There's heat and electricity. I don't like to ride for free."

She leans across my shoulder and kisses me on the cheek and says, "When they balance up the books, Flannery, I have a feeling that you're going to be very heavy in the credit column," just as Mary comes lumbering back into the kitchen asking can she have a cup of herb tea, with my old man right behind her.

"Well, what's going on here behind my back? Washing dishes, is it?" Mary says as she sits down in a kitchen chair.

"Watch out if I ever decide to change my style," Janet says, laughing her big laugh.

"That's one of the nice things about a woman of your

persuasion," Mike says. "Your girlfriends don't have to worry about their husbands."

Janet goes up behind Mike and hugs him—in her heels she's a little taller than he is—and lays a kiss on his ear.

"Haven't you heard, the leopard sometimes changes its spots if tempted sufficiently. Besides, I've always had a secret yen for fair-skinned Irishmen, and . . ."

"And what?" he says.

"Don't forget the powerful attraction ladies of any and all persuasions have about older men. Every woman in the world is looking for her daddy, one way or another."

6

I START PUTTING OUT THE WORD THE NEXT
day that I'm going to have office hours in the storefront
the next Monday and every Monday thereafter and so
on between the hours of six o'clock in the evening and
whenever.

I stop over to the Twelfth police station on Racine to
see if maybe I can get Rourke alone and have a decent
conversation without O'Shea accusing me of murdering
the man who was doing jumping jacks and leg stretches
in front of me at the Paradise. Or maybe my friend
Benedetto can give me a little information.

I catch him at the coffee urn pouring hisself a mug.

"You want some coffee, Flannery?" he asks.

"Make it half a cup," I says, not really wanting any
coffee but saying "okay, I'll have some" because that's
one of the little rituals people go through to show how
cordial they are toward one another.

There's no mugs for visitors. He half fills one of them
Styrofoam cups—which are taking over the landfills—
with black coffee and shoves it over to me with a blunt
finger. "You do your own cream and sugar."

I put in a spoonful of that coffee whitener which looks like chalk and a shot of that sweetener what comes in a pink packet and give it a stir with one of them little miniature tongue depressors.

Benedetto's watching every move I make like I'm performing brain surgery.

"It's a quarter for a cup of coffee," he says, and then, before I can dig in my pocket for some change, he tosses a quarter in the cup and says, "Forget about it. On me."

I notice, however, that he don't toss in a quarter for his own coffee so maybe the cops got an arrangement among themselves.

"You down here with a special interest," he asks, "or are you just touching bases now that you're up there with the power elite?"

"What's this power elite?" I asks.

"Well, I read this article in the paper. The power elite is the people what run the town. I mean what have we got, fifty wards in the city?"

"And thirty out in the suburbs, yeah."

"So, you're one of eighty people running the politics of the city."

"Hey," I says, warning him off all this exaggeration.

"I mean at the ward level," he says real quick. "I mean you're one of fifty city committeemen. You're a warlord."

"For God's sake, Benedetto. Either you're pulling my leg or buttering me up. One way or the other you're giving me a helluva beating."

He grins. "So, okay, what can I do you for?"

"That man what died over to the Paradise Health Spa," I says. "Did they ever get an identification on him?"

"What'd he die of?"

"Just keeled over. Well, I mean he was doing the exercises, some hip rolls and leg lifts—we was on our backs, you understand—and he never got up. So he didn't actually keel over, he just never got up."

"Heart attack. Sounds like heart attack."

"That's what I think it was, too."

"So, I'd have to look it up. I mean somebody keels over—don't get up—with a heart attack, it's not exactly a notable event. You understand what I'm saying?"

We stand there sipping the coffee. I'm waiting for him to go look it up and he's just looking at me over the rim of his mug.

"Okay," I says. "Are you going to go take a look?"

"The usual terms?"

"Hey, Benedetto," I says. "I understand how you like to trade favor for favor—how you like to keep books—but between us we don't have to bother. I mean, you don't have to have a credit from me on the books. All you got to do is ask."

"No paybacks in future? No tit for tat later on?"

. "That's right."

"Well, see, right there. That's the way the power elite operates. That's what this article said. The power elite don't make trades. They just go around doing things for people, doing them favors, no strings attached. Makes them feel powerful, is what the article says. So if one of the power elite does a favor for free, it ain't really for free. You understand what I'm saying? However . . ."

"Yeah? However, what?"

"However, people *want* to do favors back for them. Sometimes people want to do favors for them even when they don't want a favor."

"Why's that?"

"To curry favor."

"Curry," I says, wondering where Benedetto's getting all this language.

"So, what do you think? If I do this favor for you, will you think I'm trying to curry favor?"

"I'm thinking maybe I should've paid for my own coffee, then I wouldn't have to stand here and listen to this. What are you trying to say? You need a favor?"

"I could use one."

"So, tell me."

"My Carole had her appendix out."

"I'm sorry to hear that. She's okay?"

"Oh, sure. But what it is, after she come out of the hospital—what, three days?—she can't do any lifting, any heavy housework. So I get somebody to come in to help her clean. Do the heavy stuff. Two days a week. I got this woman. This young girl, really."

"She Hispanic?"

"Yeah."

"She illegal?"

"I don't know. I didn't ask her."

"You're supposed to see the green card, you hire Hispanics."

"That's for businesses with more than a certain numbers of employees."

"Even so, a cop don't want to be doing nothing illegal."

"Give me a break, Flannery. Now it's you pulling my leg."

"Speaking of which, could we sit down and get off our feet?"

"You want a refill?" he asks.

"I'm good."

He gives hisself a refill and then he gives me a look. I toss a quarter in the cup and we go sit down by his desk.

"Go ahead," I says.

"I don't know if Maria's illegal, but I can tell you she's pregnant. She had a little sick spell the other after-

noon while I was there for a minute around lunch time,
and she told me she was going to have a baby. I thought
she was just overweight."

"She got any other kids?"

"Two, I think."

"She got a husband?"

"I ain't got around to doing an interrogation on her."

"I'm only trying to get the facts here, Benedetto. I
ain't making any judgment calls."

"I thought maybe you was going to give me that old
song and dance about how a woman like Maria shouldn't
be getting knocked up all the time."

"Well, how do you feel about that? You think she
should be having all these kids? How old you say she
was?"

"She's maybe twenty. And, no, I don't think these
kids should be having all these kids, but she works for
us two days a week and my wife and me like her and
she needs to be under a doctor's care and she ain't
because she can't afford it and she says she don't qualify
for any kind of social program."

"I don't think it's such a good idea them having all
these kids either, but that don't mean I think I got anything to say about it," I says. "She don't have to pass
any means test with me. I don't know her yet but I like
her too because she's a person trying to do her best.
She's a person what needs help and that's all I care
about. So, let me ask you, you live here in the Twelfth
Police District?"

"Sure I do. Don't you know that by now?"

"You live in the Twenty-seventh Ward?"

"No, I live in the First Ward."

"Does this girl what cleans your house once a week
live in the Twenty-seventh Ward?"

"I think so. I don't know. How would I know?"

"You're a cop."

"Oh," he says.

"Have you talked to your precinct captain about this?" I asks.

"Why would I want to talk to a precinct captain when I can talk to a ward leader?"

"Because you don't want to hurt the precinct captain's feelings. You don't want to make it look like he ain't doing his job. Who's your captain?"

"Lonny Toomis."

"He did a little boxing, you know?"

"Once upon a time."

"They used to call him the Chocolate Drop?"

"That's right."

"You got his number?"

"Yeah, I got his number."

"So, you give him a call, tell him what the problem is"—I hold up my hand because I can see he's about to accuse me of ducking the issue—"and you tell him to bring the young woman to Janet Canarias's headquarters over on Gaylord Street. You know where that is?"

"Fachrissakes, Flannery, this might be your ward but part of it's in my district and I know where the alderwoman's storefront is."

"All right, then. What I'm saying is, you tell Toomis to bring Maria with him on Monday night, six o'clock, and I'll take down the particulars personally. How's that?"

He thinks about that for a minute and then he says, "Okay. By the way, you didn't have to put a quarter in the cup for my coffee. We got an arrangement between ourselves, we toss in once a week."

"So, let's just say I paid for my cup."

"But I already tossed in a quarter for your cup."

"For God's sake, Benedetto, will you look it up—what I asked you to look up—and let me get out of here?"

He goes over to the filing cabinet, opens a drawer, and

roots around before pulling a folder. He gives it a quick look, glances at me, then looks over to Captain Pescaro's office, which you can see into because the wall and door's got big glass windows in it.

Pescaro's in there bent over his desk, eyes down, up to his neck in paperwork. Benedetto closes the drawer and takes a step toward me. Pescaro raises his head. When Benedetto takes a look his way again, Pescaro points to him, points to me, and crooks his finger.

There's very little slips by under Pescaro's nose.

I follow Benedetto into the captain's office.

Pescaro stands up and extends his hand, which is a cordial gesture I ain't used to from him.

"Glad to see you, Mr. Committeeman. I was going to give you a call, offer my congratulations, but ..." He makes a motion at his cluttered desk, telling me how much work he's got piled up.

He reaches out a hand for the file, which Benedetto gives him, and says, "You giving Mr. Flannery a little cooperation here, Benedetto?"

"He had a couple of harmless questions," Benedetto says, ready to cover hisself.

"No need to explain, Anthony. We're always ready to cooperate with the ward leader."

This is a considerable change in attitude. Usually Pescaro accuses me of sticking my nose in where it don't belong, interfering with police business, and generally making a pain in the ass out of myself.

"Have a chair. Both of you. Let's see what we can do for you, Jim." He does a quick take on the file which has only got a couple pages in it. "Uh-huh, uh-huh, uh-huh," he says. "What do you want to know?"

"I was just wondering if you found out who the man was that dropped dead—"

"Never got up off the floor, actually," Benedetto says.

"—over to the Paradise Health Spa."

"We haven't."

I don't say anything, but I suppose I pop my eyebrows a little bit.

"We're making an effort," Pescaro says. "But we're not throwing out any dragnets. Sooner or later a missing person report'll come in and we'll make a match and then we'll know."

I can see he's a little irritated having to explain, but he's doing it because we've got this new relationship going here and we might as well get off on the right foot. I can see that being a ward leader ain't so bad.

"I was just curious," I says.

"I wouldn't expect anything less of a conscientious man like yourself," Pescaro says. "Anything else we can help you with?"

"I was wondering about the autopsy."

He lifts two pages stapled together.

"Routine. Heart attack. You got doubts?"

"Well, you know, the way he went. So sudden."

"That's how it goes with heart attacks. He was exercising. He was a heavyweight doing strenuous exercises, ain't that right? A man that weight, that age, should take it slow. That's the way it happens." He snaps his fingers showing how fast it happens. "A man that age, that weight, doing strenuous exercises."

"I was wondering about his eyes."

"His eyes?"

"They was half open when I took a look at him. I could see there was like a little rim of bluish white stuff around the iris. You know what I mean? Like the milky cataracts old men and old dog's get."

He scans the autopsy report again.

"No mention of cataracts. Maybe the man wore contact lenses. Maybe what you saw was an optical illusion. Like a reflection."

"Does it say he wore contacts?"

"This is just a preliminary report. Just what was put down at the scene. This ain't the postmortem."

"It was nothing important," I says, getting to my feet. "I just wondered, that's all."

Pescaro gets up, too. "We had more conscientious citizens and public servants like you, Jim, we'd be in much better shape."

"I could say the same about you," I says, giving him the compliment right back.

"On the subject . . ." he says.

I wait for what subject he's talking about. Maybe a pleasant little reminder—not like some of his reminders in the past—that I should butt out and let the police do the job they're getting paid for. But instead he nearly knocks me over when he says, "Jim, in a case like this we could maybe use a little help from somebody like yourself who's got a large organization at his disposal. There ain't enough hours in the day for us to do everything we got to do, so when something like this dead man in the gym comes along—a man what died by natural causes but who ain't got any identification on him and no mention so far that anybody's noticed he's gone missing and all—we ain't got enough men to put on the streets, knocking on doors and doing what it takes to run down a missing person."

"You want me to help?"

"I'm thinking maybe now that you're the ward committeeman, you could have a word with your precinct captains and tell them to keep an ear out for any talk of a man who didn't come home Saturday night. You might even suggest they could ask around about such a missing person. You know, in the taverns and barber shops and beauty parlors, where the people go to drink, get their hair done, gossip, and hang out. Could you do that?"

"I could and will, Captain Pescaro."

"Call me Dominick. Better yet, call me Dom. I guess only my mama ever called me Dominick. My mama and my wife when she's mad at me."

"My mother—God bless her soul—and my wife are the only ones ever called me James," I says.

We shake hands again. He walks me to the door. I can hardly stand all the cordiality.

7

ALTHOUGH DELVIN'S HANDED ME THE PALM in the Democratic Party regular organization when he decides to retire as committeeman of the Twenty-seventh, he's still my boss in the Department of Sewers.

He gives me a week off to set up the way I'm going to run the ward—which some people might say is just another example of political graft and others might say is just a perk to a man working two jobs for one paycheck—but I want to start off on the right foot, so I take the week but insist it's charged against the sick time I got coming to me.

The job of organizing my ward operation ain't that complicated or time consuming. I already know most of the people I'm going to be doing business with, so all I'm really doing is going around shaking hands.

Most everybody seems genuinely happy that I got the ward leadership and that makes me very happy. Among other people I stop by to see is my old childhood friend, Eddie Fergusen, who's still working down at the morgue.

I go down on Thursday to get his congratulations, and

since I'm already there, I ask him a couple of questions.

"You got another name for this P. Pig yet?" I asks.

"For who? For what?" he says.

"A man was brought in here Saturday night."

"A dozen men and about the same number of women was brought in here Saturday night. At least that many. Shot, stabbed, poisoned, beaten to death, and otherwise abused."

"Well, this one came in dead of heart attack, I think."

Eddie's going through the list for Saturday.

"There's a Mr. Porky here. That's the closest thing we got to a P. Pig," he says.

"I'd say that was probably him. The attendant heard the name wrong or wrote it down wrong."

"That's more than possible," he says. "Uh-oh."

"What's with the 'uh-oh'?" I says.

"They started a file on him."

"So, you'll take a minute and pull it?"

"A red-cover file."

"What's with this red-cover file business?"

"Confidential."

"That shouldn't bother us."

"Locked up, Jimmy. Locked up where I can't get at it."

"Locked up why and by who?"

"I'd say by Dr. Hackman, the medical examiner."

"I know Dr. Hackman very well," I says.

"Well, if you know him very well, then you know him better than I do. So you want to ask him about the red-cover file, you go on in and ask him."

"Is he working?"

"He's practically always working. That don't bother him. Go ahead. I'll buzz you through. You know the way?"

"I been there before," I says.

He hits the buzzer under the counter which unlocks

the door to the corridor that leads to various offices and storerooms and the laboratory where they do the autopsies. The rubber heels on my shoes squeak as I walk along. I'm not really enjoying the prospect of talking to Hackman while he's up to his elbows in somebody's belly or sawing off the top of somebody's head. It didn't used to be that way. I mean, I didn't think it was a joy being around dead people—especially them what died violently—but it bothers me more nowadays and I guess that's part of what comes with growing old. Hackman once told me that you never really get used to it, cutting up bodies the way he's done for years and years, it just gets harder and harder. It gets so you're afraid that you'll start seeing yourself there under the knife and you got to try very hard to turn your mind's eye away.

So I practice turning my mind's eye away and there I am in the autopsy room picking up a molded protective paper mask and walking up to Hackman who's working on a naked young Hispanic woman with a swollen face laying on the table. He's working alone, dictating into the overhead mike as he goes along. When he hears my footsteps, he glances up, pauses, and drapes her face with a towel. Hackman's very careful about showing respect for the dead.

"It's a closed file, Flannery," he says before I say a word.

"What's a closed file?" I says through the mask which I'm holding against my mouth and nose.

"The report on Mr. Porky, the man who was brought in with an apparent heart attack suffered while exercising in a health spa."

"I was there. I was right behind him, doing the exercises."

"I know. Your name was on the report as witness to

the death. How do you think I knew this wasn't just a social visit?"

"You said 'apparent heart attack.' What does that mean?"

"It means I don't know everything I'd like to know yet."

"Like what?"

"Just as I thought," he says, not answering me because he has no intention of answering me. "This young woman died of septicemia caused by a botched abortion."

"How's that?" I says, showing some interest, waiting for a chance to get in another question about Mr. Porky.

"I mean that somebody destroyed the fetus by means of a wire coat hanger or a dirty scraper and this young woman died of a massive infection."

"She wasn't beat to death?"

"Her face?"

"I caught a glimpse."

"That was where the infection ended up, in the gums and the lymph system that drains through the upper part of the head. Nothing's simple, is it, Jimmy? Nothing's what it seems."

"Like Mr. Porky and his heart attack," I says.

"Like that," he says, giving me a look.

He drapes the entire body with a sheet and walks over to the shrouded body on the next table, peeling off his gloves as he goes. He flicks the sheet off the face, takes a look and flicks it back.

"This is a gun shot. It'll take some time. Cigarette break."

He walks across the laboratory and goes into a big closet with shelves piled with sheets. There's a table with an ash tray on it and a couple of chairs.

I'm still thinking about the girl dying of an abortion.

"How come?" I asks.

"How come what?"

"The young girl in there."

"How come she died of a botched abortion? Because they don't get the proper advice. Because they don't know abortion's available even if they haven't got the price. Because they hear all the business on television about state and federal court decisions and they don't quite get the meaning. So they get bad advice or no advice and maybe they're illegals—no green card—so they try it the old way, the hard way. And they die," he says.

"They knock out the availability of abortion on demand," he goes on, "and they refuse to fund birth control clinics and products, and the next thing you know, it'll be back to the good old days. Back-alley abortions everywhere and girls like that one in there dying of it. Ahh, why go on about it?" he says.

He lights up a cigarette after offering me one which I refuse.

"I still don't understand why Mr. Porkey's file was put in a red cover," I says, taking another shot at it.

There's just a half a tick of hesitation while Hackman balances out some conflict and then he says, "Because somebody of some importance requested it."

"To keep a heart attack secret? Come on."

"You're a persistent man, Flannery."

"Some people say I hold on like a junkyard dog."

"Well, I'm one old bone you're going to break your teeth on. I've got no reason to tell you anything, Jimmy. You're not a cop. You're not a member of the man's family."

"Well, that's right," I says. "I hardly knew the man, but the way it looks, I could turn out being his only friend. The only person who cares to know how he died."

8

I'VE GOT A FRIEND, ABE GRESHIN, OWNS A COIN and stamp shop up on the avenue next to the drug store.

He's very happy to see me when I walk through the door.

"So, here he is, the big *macher*, the committeeman, the next alderman of the Twenty-seventh, the mayor, the governor—"

"Hey, hey, hey, that's enough," I says, going along with the joke. "Hey, don't make me president. They tell me the summers back in Washington, D.C., are worse than Chicago's."

"Ah, my boy, I can't tell you how proud I am of you," he says, coming around the counter and giving me a hug.

Abe's wearing the usual suit and tie—which he says matches the dignity of the trade he's in—but on his feet he's got the oldest pair of carpet slippers in town.

When I glance down to see they ain't been buried, he

looks down, too, and says, "Sometimes comfort is more important than appearances. So, come, sit down and tell me how's your lovely wife and the child-to-be."

"They're both getting along fine according to the doctors," I says, sitting on the customer's stool at the long glass case which is the counter.

"God bless them both," he says, taking his usual place on the other side. "You got a question or did you just stop by to chew the fat?"

I take the coin, which is a five-lire piece, from my pocket and put it on the piece of green cloth he uses for display and examination.

"Oh, sure, you've got a Victor Emmanuel the Third there."

"Is it worth anything?"

"Book value, a hundred dollars."

"Book value?"

"That's an estimate they put in the catalogs to make collectors feel rich."

"So, what's it worth?"

"I can sell you one for sixty dollars. I'll buy one for forty. You going to be a collector?"

"It's not one of my interests."

"I wondered. Some people, when they have a baby, start collecting coins like a savings account. You buy right, not only can you keep out ahead of inflation and do better than bank interest, but you can keep out in front of most investments. You should think about it. You got a start right here."

"Well, this coin ain't mine," I says.

"You're doing an estimation for a friend?"

"Sort of."

"This the only one?"

"There was four others."

"Can you bring them in?"

"That'd be hard to do."

He shrugs. So that's all he can do for me, it says.

"Maybe I can remember the others," I says.

"Try."

"There was five coins, four five-lire pieces and one ten-lire piece," I says, closing my eyes and calling up the picture of Dugan turning them over in his palm.

"Thirty lire in silver," Abe says, and looks at me over the tops of his glasses. "Thirty pieces of silver?"

He's asking if the coins got something to do with a betrayal. He's very quick, Abe is, and knows I wouldn't be bothering him asking about a coin unless there was something more than just its value involved.

"If you want to put it that way," I says.

"Okay, so we got this coin and four others," he says.

"There's a five-lire coin with horses on it."

"You remember the date?"

"Sure, 1914. That was easy to remember. There's two with eagles, one minted in 1927, the other in—I think—1930."

He's checking his own memory in a little catalogue and making notes on a slip of paper.

"The ten-lire piece also had 1930 on it," I says.

"Victor's face again," he says. "So what we got—book price—is a hundred and fifty for the horses . . ."

I'm beginning to think what we got here is maybe a coin theft which got Mr. Porky killed.

". . . the 1927 is worth one and a half, the five-lire, 1930, two and a half and the ten-lire, six."

"Hundred dollars?"

"Bucks. One and a half bucks. Two and a half bucks. Six bucks. Catalogue. You thought you was rich there for a minute, didn't you? I could see the gleam of the collector in your eye."

"Well, easy come, easy go," I says.

Adding it up on my fingers I got a total of two hundred sixty dollars. A third of that if you're selling, not buying. Not a fortune.

"There a lot of these floating around?" I asks.

"Not tons but enough," Abe says. "You sure I can't interest you in a nice 1908 twenty-dollar gold piece to start the baby's college education fund?"

9

I GO TO A PHOTOGRAPHER FRIEND OF MINE
and have the picture of Mr. Porky copied sixty times,
then I go hand one out to every one of my precinct
captains and tell them to ask around about this missing
man in his early to middle fifties, fat and going bald,
who's probably Italian and maybe can even speak the
language and who—maybe—has been to the old country
not too long ago. I mention that they don't have to
worry about getting static from the cops since Pescaro
hisself asks me to help them out.

I also get on the telephone and ask Jerry Kilian, the
committeeman from the First, if he'll ask his precinct
captains to do the same. I tell him I'll stop by wherever
he wants to meet and give him some pictures.

"Is there something fishy about the death of this
man?" Kilian asks.

"How do you mean fishy?" I asks.

"I mean criminal, illegal, illicit, or immoral."

"What seems to be the problem, doing me this little
favor?"

"No problem. I'm just asking. Maybe I'm nervous

about unidentified men dropping dead ever since they found that stiff over to Molly Danaher's upstairs bedroom and it turns out it's Father Harrigan commuting in for a little R and R from a parish in Cicero."

"I don't think this is nothing like that. I can guarantee you that he didn't die while amorously engaged because I was doing jumping jacks right behind him not ten feet away."

"Jumping jacks?" Kilian says with this little bolt of concern in his voice.

"Exercises, Jerry. Exercises."

"Well, okay. So, how's it feel being a general instead of a foot soldier?"

"I already got the feeling I ain't going to have the time I used to have just going around chewing the fat with my friends and neighbors."

"I know what you mean."

"I got the feeling I'm going to get pinned down behind a desk and a telephone somewhere telling other people what to do instead of doing it myself."

"Well, that happens, but you got to remember there's no book of rules about how you want to run your ward as long as you deliver the votes on election day. So you want to be a delegator, be a delegator. You want to be a doer, be a doer. You got yourself an office where your captains and the people can come for a talk?"

"I'm available to my captains at Brennan's every Saturday afternoon and Janet Canarias's giving me the use of her storefront every Monday night."

"You got a good relationship with the alderwoman, then?"

"She's my wife's best friend."

"She's very smart, very able, is Janet Canarias," Kilian says. "She could go on to bigger and better things if she plays her cards right."

"I don't think she's ever thought of going for higher office."

"I wasn't talking city, you understand. I was talking state."

"Oh, sure, I know that's what you were talking but, except for governor or maybe the attorney general, there's nothing higher in state government than a Chicago alderman," I says.

"I'm just saying maybe you should put a bug in her ear all the same. You never know."

"So, thanks in front for helping me out on this other thing," I says.

"My pleasure. I know you'd do the same for me if I ever needed it."

He says good-bye and hangs up and I do the same. I sit there thinking about how Kilian was suggesting I should give Janet a little nudge—seeing as how I was so friendly with her—so she'll start thinking about state office. Get her out of town. Get the Twenty-seventh back for the regular Democratic organization with yours truly maybe being the candidate.

So, for right now, that's the only ward leader I call about asking around about a missing, middle-aged Italian because I'm betting on the fact that Mr. Porky lived somewhere in the Twenty-seventh or the First so it wouldn't be a lot of trouble getting to the Paradise for the exercise he was taking to lose a little weight.

By the time Monday rolls around I ain't heard word one about the real identity of Mr. Porky or any news of a missing man that fits in the slightest the rough description I gave out.

Somebody's made a neatly lettered sign that says "Committeeman James Flannery—Available For Questions Or Consultations," and stuck it in the window of the storefront. The lights are on and the door's unlocked.

So even though I'm very early, it looks like somebody's already there before me.

Dan McGuire and Packy Cooley come walking toward me when I come through the door. Cooley's the first to stick out his hand and McGuire's the second—which comes as something of a surprise. Millie Jefferson, sitting on a wooden bench with a young black girl who's already showing big, and Helen Reeba, who's standing beside an old woman also sitting on the bench, smile at me and come over to greet me, too.

Millie kisses me on the cheek and murmurs, "Hey, Jimmy, Helen was going to nominate me and I was going to nominate her, but we didn't mean it serious, you understand? We just wanted to make the point."

I kiss her back. "You should've done it and been serious."

"We would've voted for you anyway," Helen says. "So, you ready to do business? I put a pot of coffee in the office."

"I don't want to mess up the alderwoman's desk," I says.

"I don't think she'd care, we serve a little coffee. But when we went to get the key so we could be here when you came, we told her we thought you'd be more comfortable using the little office and she said that was just like you."

"That's good."

"So, there's coffee," Helen says. "Millie wanted to put in a plate of doughnuts, too, but Ms. Canarias said we'd better not. You was on a diet and the temptation could be too great."

"I don't know. It'd be nice if I could offer anybody who comes to see me a little something. I mean, for God's sake, I think I can resist a doughnut."

"Even a sticky?"

"Even a sticky with chocolate glaze."

"Millie gives Helen a look like she's won a bet and says, "See? I'll just go out to my car and get the box."

"I want to pay for them," I call after her.

"Next time. You'll pay next time," Millie says as she goes out the door.

"This first time is on us," Helen says. "Go on in and sit down. You might as well get started."

"Could you give me a minute? I'd like to talk to Dan for a minute."

I ask McGuire to come with me into the little side office Janet's assistant and office administrator uses. I offer him a chair and I go sit down behind the desk.

It feels very funny sitting behind a desk. Usually I'm on the other side. There's a world of difference.

McGuire don't look too comfortable either.

"I don't suppose it feels very natural to you, me being the committeeman instead of Delvin," I says.

"Well, the old man was around for a long time. It's going to take some getting used to, looking at another face."

"The old man's still around, you ever want to have a talk for old times sake, you ever come up against something you don't think you could feel comfortable talking to me about. I ain't going to jump into his shoes and try to pretend I'm him."

"I'm glad to hear that."

"Also I want you to know that I understand about loyalty and how hard it dies."

He's looking me in the eye. Even though it sounds like we're talking about Delvin, we ain't really talking about him anymore. We're talking about McGuire's friendship with Baily, who's doing time in state for second degree murder.

"I admire a man who sticks by his friends, Dan," I says. "You ever go up to visit Big Buck?"

He looks startled.

"I go up maybe once a month. Between times I send

him cigarettes, candy, shaving stuff. You know. Like he was in the army."

"It was wrong what he did, killing them two gays."

"He was drunk."

"That's the great excuse, ain't it? A man's drunk, he don't have any control over what he does. Diminished capacity, they call it. Lawyers use it for a defense all the time. Well, maybe so, but I'm asking you, Dan, if you was drunk, do you think you could beat some poor gamoosh to death with your fists?"

"I don't think so," he says, after a long pause.

"I don't think so either," I says. "Because it ain't in you. And I don't think it's in you to hold a grudge either. I did what I had to do, Dan, and I wasn't drunk when I did it. I went after Baily and Connel because what they did was wrong. What they did was a danger to everybody. On top of which they tried to blame it on Baby, the gorilla what was Chicago's pet. You understand what I'm saying here, Dan?"

"I think so."

"I'm saying I'd like to let bygones be bygones. I'm saying I understand that we maybe can't be the best of friends, but we can be cordial when we meet."

"I'd like to try that," he says.

I stand up and reach out to shake his hand as he stands up, too. "Okay, then. You want to be my sergeant at arms tonight? You want to see that everybody stays orderly in case we get a crowd? You want to ask Helen Reeba to come on in with that old lady?"

McGuire brightens right up. He leaves the office and a minute later he opens the door and ushers Helen and the old lady—who must be eighty, ninety—into the office.

"This is Mrs. Carmen Quintana. She's going to have a baby," Helen says.

10

HELEN REEBA'S A GIGGLER. SHE'S GOT THIS beautiful, round, dusky, rosy face and six kids with the same round, dusky, rosy faces. She's been working for the Democratic Party for six years, walking her neighborhood, sometimes going around at night in places which are not all that safe. Her and my old man get along very well, having conversations that you could call dueling adages or maxims or whatever they call these sayings that are supposed to sum things up.

Like he'll say to her "Trust everybody but don't be disappointed if they kick you in the keister," and she'll say, "You can't know the blisters I got unless you walk a mile in my shoes."

She'll say something like that or he'll say something like that and she'll giggle. It's the kind of giggle you can't help laughing yourself. So Helen starts in and the next thing you know everybody in the room is laughing.

So she tells me Mrs. Quintana is going to have a baby and then she starts giggling, and Mrs. Quintana's dear, old face wrinkles up like a withered apple as she starts giggling, and the next thing I know I'm laughing, too.

"I don't mean that Great-grandmother's having a baby. I mean her great-granddaughter Rosa is going to have a baby," Helen says.

"Well, that's a relief," I says. "I was just about to pick up the phone and call the newspapers, call the television, call Ripley."

I was talking a little too fast for Great-grandma to catch my English so Helen does a quick translation.

The old lady frowns and says something back in Spanish. All I catch is Ripley.

"She doesn't understand who is this Ripley."

"Oh?"

"I don't know what this Ripley is either, Jimmy."

"Well, it don't matter. You can tell her later that Ripley was a man collected stories and facts about unusual people like herself. I mean like herself would be if she was the one having the baby at her age."

Helen says something that seems to satisfy Mrs. Quintana for the minute, even though she still looks puzzled.

"How can I help you?" I asks.

"Mrs. Quintana is very old," Helen says.

"Yes, I can see that. Very old and very beautiful."

"I'll save that for later, too, Jimmy. The fact is that she had her babies on a dirt floor and so did her daughters. But one of her granddaughters came up here and brought Mrs. Quintana north first chance she could. Mrs. Quintana has her granddaughter and her great-grandchildren read to her. She has them read to her about medicine and good health. She understands pre-natal care which would have prevented some of her own babies from dying and the babies of her daughters from dying. Well, she says, even up here in the States, babies are dying. Her great-granddaughter, Rosa, is seven months pregnant and she can't get a doctor to take care of her."

"Is she on welfare?"

"Mrs. Quintana?"

"Well, her and anybody else in the family."

"Her granddaughter works off the books. Can I tell you that?"

"As long as they make it so that a poor person what wants to work gets penalized for working, you can tell me that."

"How about Rosa, the girl having the baby?"

"She's fifteen."

"So, she's in school?"

"No, she's a dropout. She was working in a five-and-ten for minimum wages until she started showing very big. Now, she's staying at home. Mrs. Quintana's worried about her. She don't get no exercise. She sits around putting on too much weight, eating too much, smoking *hierba*—you know?—and drinking wine."

"She shouldn't be doing that," I says.

"Mrs. Quintana knows that, I know that, and you know that. So, go tell that to a fifteen-year-old. Somebody with authority's got to talk to her. A doctor."

"Or a nurse."

"If she knows what she's talking about and ain't too harsh."

"Oh, she knows what she's talking about and she's got plenty of sympathy. My wife Mary used to work for an abortion clinic. She volunteered her time."

Mrs. Quintana must've understood the word *abortion* and it scares her, because she crosses herself and shakes her head very hard.

"Tell her I'm not suggesting that Rosa gets rid of the baby. I'm just saying that my wife volunteered her time because she believes that a woman has a right to make that decision about should she end a pregnancy she didn't ask for."

Helen rattles off some Spanish and the old lady rattles off some right back.

"She says the child is only fifteen. How can she be expected to make such a decision?"

I'm afraid I'm getting into deep water here.

"I didn't say that she could or should. I was just trying to make it plain that my wife has a great deal of sympathy for mothers-to-be. She's going to have a baby herself."

"I didn't know this, Jimmy," Helen says.

"Oh, yes, she's about seven months herself."

Helen gets up, comes around the desk, and kisses me on the cheek.

"You give that to your wife," she says.

"I tell my wife pretty women are coming up to me and giving me kisses, I don't know how she'll take it."

Helen giggles, knowing that I'm teasing her. Mrs. Quintana laughs because Helen's laughing. So I laugh just to go along and because I can't help myself and because it feels so good.

"Anyway, Mary's putting in some volunteer hours at a free prenatal clinic at the Mary Thompson Hospital every Wednesday and Friday evening. You know where that is?"

"Over on Ashland and Washington."

"That's right. I'll write it down anyway in case somebody besides yourself takes Mrs. Quintana and Rosa over there. All they got to do is show this to whoever's at the desk and they'll show the girl right in to see my wife. I'll tell her about it tonight or tomorrow at breakfast. Okay?"

Helen rattles off some more Spanish which tells the old lady enough so that her old face wrinkles up in this great smile and tears come to her eyes.

I stand up. "Will you ask Ms. Jefferson to come in with her client now?"

The ladies stand up and Mrs. Quintana grabs my hand and tries to kiss it as I walk them to the door.

"Oh, gee, tell her she shouldn't do that, Helen," I

says, but I don't snatch my hand away because I don't want to insult the old lady.

"It's the custom of her country to thank the *patrono*," Helen says.

"I understand that, but this is her country now and I ain't a *patrono* and she don't have to do that sort of thing anymore."

"She knows she don't *have* to do it, Jimmy. She *wants* to do it."

The old lady's holding my hand and smiling up into my face like she understands what Helen's saying. Then she reaches up and pats my cheek like I was a kid, so I bend down a little and kiss her on the cheek.

"She's worried about her family," Helen says. "She tells me she's going to die soon and she worries about what will happen to them without her."

"Oh, my," I says, because I don't know what else to say.

11

WHEN MILLIE JEFFERSON COMES IN, SHEP-
herding this pregnant chocolate brown girl in front of
her, I get a feeling I'm about to hear more of the same—
how hard it is to get the system to deliver what they're
supposed to deliver—and I'm right.

"A girl like Hester here just can't make her way
through the red tape," Millie says.

"You give her a hand?"

"I give her a couple of days. I walk through the system
with her. But I tell you, it's almost as hard for me as it
is for her. I went and got some facts."

Millie goes into her big carryall. Millie Jefferson's a
little woman about thirty-five years old. Weight a hundred pounds soaking wet like my old man would say.
She's got a little pointy face, reminds you of a fox, and
this reddish-black hair what tells you she douses it with
henna the way some of the ladies like to do. This carryall she totes around looks to be about half as big as she
is and it must weigh a ton. I picked it up one time and
I know.

You wouldn't believe what comes out of that carryall sometimes. This time a little calculator's in her hand. At least I think it's a calculator until she tells me that what she's got there is an electronic notebook. Her kids and her husband chipped in and got her one for her birthday so she can keep her busy schedule straight and do all sorts of other things.

Like now she taps it a couple of times and starts reading from its little screen.

"There's two hundred patients a day—average—stuffed into every city and county clinic. I went and sat and counted. I had other people go and sit and count."

She looks at me, waiting for my reaction. I shake my head.

"Some patients bring their lunch and sleep in the corridors. They know how long a wait they're looking at. How long you think? It's not unusual they got to wait eight hours for a prescription to be filled."

She looks at me again. I shrug my shoulders and make a face like this information is giving me pain.

What she don't know is that Mary's giving me these kind of statistics all the time.

Just the other day she tells me a story how this woman's brought in with labor pains two o'clock in the morning over to Passavant where Mary still puts in some part-time during the day. So she wasn't actually there, but a friend tells her how they examine this woman and find complications that would've been prevented if she'd had the kind of prenatal care she should've had. All she's had is one ultrasound over to St. Francis Cabrini. That's some time ago and now's now, but because she's already had the examination over to Cabrini, more than a mile away, that's where they send her. On foot.

Instead of admitting her, Cabrini ships her over to Holy Cross who won't admit her either. They bounce her over to Northwestern Memorial. Finally she gets sent to Cook County where they got to take her. She has the baby and it's okay but there's been other times when it wasn't okay.

"Half the women presenting at other hospitals and transferred to Cook County were too far along in labor to be safely and legally transferred," Millie goes on. "You understand what I'm saying here, Jimmy?"

"You're describing to me a system what ain't working too good."

"I'm describing a system that's killing babies. Right here it says that fifty-nine hundred babies were born at County in '88 and a hundred and seventy-five of them died. That mortality rate's worse than Romania, for God's sake. Worse than Malaysia or Trinidad."

"I know where Trinidad is," Hester says brightly. "My mother says that my father come from Trinidad. Sweet-talking men in Trinidad."

Millie looks at the girl like she's gone crazy right before our eyes.

"Never mind sweet-talking men. We know you can tell us something about sweet-talking men. What we're talking about here is what women got to do after they been listening to sweet-talking men." Millie looks at me like I'm one of them sweet-talking villains myself.

I figure I've got to cut this interview short before Millie blames me for something I didn't do.

"So, what you want is for me to see if I can get Hester some care and advice," I says.

"Well, somebody has to have some influence with these people. It's been made pretty plain to me that a precinct captain ain't got scissors big enough or sharp enough to cut through this tangled tape," Millie says.

I write down my wife's name and the address of the free prenatal clinic on a piece of paper, though from the look of Hester such care and advice should have been given to her long ago. And maybe a little instruction in contraception some time before that.

They leave and McGuire sticks his head in the door. He acts like he's enjoying being my sergeant at arms. Sometimes all you got to do to turn an enemy into a friend is ask him to do a favor for you which makes him feel a little important.

"You ready for another?" he asks.

"Another what?"

He turns his head, opens the door a little wider and makes a move with his arm as though he's gathering Lonny Toomis and Benedetto's pregnant maid into the fold.

It looks like I'm going to be up to my eyeballs in pregnant young ladies before the night's over with.

12

I DON'T KNOW IF I EVER MENTIONED B. BEHAN. Which is the way he's got it printed on his business cards, trying, I suppose, to make everybody think his first name is Brendan, who was this Irish writer of plays and stories and who was also a drunkard, a barroom brawler and a bisexual, the worst of which everybody's got to figure out for themselves. Anyway B. Behan's name ain't Brendan, it's Billy.

Billy Behan's about sixty years old. He calls hisself a newspaperman and a reporter—it says so right on his car—and he runs around sticking his nose into places where he ain't wanted, sniffing around for anything what smells rotten. Since I get accused of doing the same thing all the time, I can sympathize with Behan's situation except there's a difference, which maybe only I and the people who support me can see.

Which is that when I stick my nose in anywhere, I'm usually trying to help somebody out of a pickle and when Behan sticks his nose in, he's looking for something to club somebody with and he don't care if that somebody is a villain or just a person down on his or her luck trying to keep their noses above the flood. Also, he sells the information and little scandals he digs up to smut magazines, neighborhood newspapers with axes to grind and even—once or twice—the big national checkout counter tabloids that write up unproven cases of three-headed babies and six hundred pound men marrying sixty pound women. He even manages to sell a feature story to the *Trib* and *Sun-Times* now and then.

Behan, at one time or another, was a legitimate reporter for practically every daily that's been published in Chicago since he was old enough to get working papers and pound a typewriter with two fingers. But drink and a natural tendency to rub everybody the wrong way got him fired from job after job until there was no way left for him to make a living except to do what he calls free-lancing and other people call garbage picking.

The reason he can't get a regular job on the *Trib* or *Sun-Times*, he tells me whenever he backs me into a corner here or there, is because he's too close to the age when he'll be needing medical care as a result of all the hard living he's been doing and the lousy insurance companies don't want to bear the costs. So the papers won't hire him no matter how much they might want his services.

He's one of the meanest, nastiest people I ever met, but I still say hello to him every time we happen to meet even though half the time he growls at me like a junkyard dog and even tells me to go do something unnatural to myself. When people I'm with ask me how come I still try to act cordial to Behan when he gives me back what he gives me back, I tell them I have this idea that I'm not going to let anybody change my good nature or good feelings on any given day by making me react to meanness with meanness.

So who walks through the door next on this first day of me acting like a ward leader—this very important day—but Billy Behan, grinning at me like a cur what can't make up its mind if it should smile and get its belly scratched or show its teeth and bite the first hand that tries to pet it.

"Hello, Billy," I says, standing up and putting out my hand.

He shakes it, which shows just how friendly he's going to try to be. Then he sits down and says, "So you finally went and done it."

I sit down again and says, "Finally went and done what, Billy?"

"Finally went and rolled over so they'd let you have a place at the trough."

"What trough is this you're talking about?"

"The trough where the pigs glut themselves, gobbling up the goodies that rightfully belong to the people. All you politicians and ward heelers."

"Practically everybody I know calls me the ward leader or committeeman, Billy. I don't know about being a heeler. I'm not wearing anybody's leash and you goddam well know it."

"You're a loose cannon all right. I've give you that," he says, grinning like a shark or maybe a skinny barracuda. "They'll have their hands full figuring out what you'll be doing next. What *will* you be doing next, Flannery?"

"I'll be doing next what I always been doing, lending a helping hand to anybody what needs it."

He looks down at the floor and delicately plucks at the knees of his pants.

"What're you doing" I asks, knowing damn well what he's doing but giving him the pleasure of saying it, hoping another shot at me'll satisfy him and get him out of the office.

"I was thinking maybe you was laying down on your other job. I was thinking maybe the sewer backed up and was spreading out all over the floor and I didn't want it to get my cuffs and socks all wet."

"I can't help it, you got a sour stomach, Billy. I know it's hard for you to believe there's people who like to help other people. I can understand you figure that whatever anybody does, there's got to be something in it for them."

"You bet your sweet ass," Behan says. "Nobody does nothing for nothing."

"So that's okay. It makes you happy. But you asked me what I had in mind now that I'm the committeeman and I told you. If you want anything else, you're just going to have to watch and wait."

"That's exactly what I intend to do, Flannery," he says, getting to his feet.

"Is that what you stopped by for?"

"I stopped by to offer my congratulations, Flannery," he says, and for a minute there his eyes and mouth soften a little bit, "and to tell you at least one of the fourth estate is going to be doing his job, seeing to it that people sworn to help the people ain't stealing them blind."

"You ever want my help in helping you do that, all you got to do is give me a call or come right back here every Monday evening and ask."

"The only thing I ever ask is questions, Flannery," he says.

"So, that's all right, too."

13

SOME NIGHTS WHEN I GET HOME FROM WORK
or from walking the precinct—which I'm still doing
because it's a habit I can't give up, a pleasure I don't
want to give up—Mary's sitting in a straight-backed
chair by the kitchen window staring out at the back
yards of the neighborhood.

Alfie's laying at her feet with his head on his paws,
dreaming away the twilight.

I come in and hunker down on the linoleum next to
her, give Alfie a pat on the head and lay my ear on
Mary's belly, listening for our kid stirring around in
there.

I read these articles and see these programs on the
television what say that a woman is a natural parent
because she and the baby establish a relationship, flesh
to flesh and blood to blood, through nine long months,
which seems perfectly logical to me. They say that a
man has to learn how to be a parent, that it don't come
natural at all. The father ain't had no relationship with
the child before it's actually born.

Well, I don't know about that.

I got a relationship with the baby what ain't been born yet. I listen to our baby stir around and sometimes I feel our baby kick, so I already got feelings about this baby. Sometimes I talk to the baby.

Anyway I come home the middle of the week and squat down alongside Mary and put my ear on her belly and she lays her hand on my head.

"So, what kind of day?" she says.

"Millie Jefferson runs me down today and hands me the name of another pregnant, unwed minority girl, fourteen, fifteen years old. This one ain't even in the Ward."

"The director says we can't take any more referrals from all over the city," Mary says. "The clinic's already overloaded."

"I don't know if this is working out, Mary," I says.

"What's not working out?"

"This volunteer work you're putting in over to Mary Thompson Hospital. I mean you go part-time days over to Passavant because it's getting closer and closer to your time and the doctor tells you that you got to cut down, and then you go volunteering over to Mary Thompson. So what we got is we got you working two jobs instead of one and not getting enough rest at all. You're biting off more than you can chew."

"Like a certain somebody I know."

"If you're talking about me, I want you to understand that I know how far I can go and how much I can do before I keel over."

"I won't do more than I can do, James."

"You've got to promise me that, Mary. If anything happened to you, I don't know ..."

I don't even want to say what would happen to me if anything happened to her.

"I don't know what we're going to do about them,

James. All the young girls and women caught in the trap of their own feelings. I mean, there I was one time trying to do what I could do, giving them a chance to stop the process of child-bearing before they let it go too late. Giving them a chance to change things. Alter the consequences of the things they did because of all the hormones storming around inside their bodies," she says. "Now here I am trying to help the ones who want their babies to see it through, give birth to healthy children. One way and the other way it's so hard to get it right, make a difference."

"That's because of what television, all this communication, does to our heads," I says. "There was a time when all a person knew was the neighborhood, maybe a little bit about some relatives who lived twenty, thirty miles away. Anything much further than that was too far away to worry about. In regular times I mean. Not when the news of war or some disaster spread far and wide. Then the radio come along and spread the circle wider and wider. Now we got television and we got the troubles of the whole country, the whole world smacking us in the face every night at five o'clock."

"We can't pretend we don't know about it and just ignore it," Mary says.

"That's right," I says. "We just do what we can do. One at a time. First come, first served. But we also got to know when we can't do anymore because, if we try to do everything, we'll fall over in a faint and then we won't be able to do any good for anybody. And we got to know when the time comes when we can't stuff one more person into the system or it'll just break down so that everybody'll go without."

"Mrs. Kasimir, the director of the clinic at Mary Thompson, says that time's come for the clinic."

"Then we got to take her word for it, Mary. I'll stop

sending referrals until you tell me otherwise. And you got to promise me not to do so much."

She leans over to kiss me but her belly won't let her.

"If I'm going to kiss you," she says, "you've got to give me a little help."

I straighten up and she kisses me and we hold each other for a minute.

"Mike's stopping by for supper. I'd better go look at the stew," she says.

"I'll do that. Give us another minute."

She settles her head on my shoulder and we both look out across the back yards.

"I can remember when I was a little kid," I says. "The women in the old neighborhood had clothes washers, most of them, but only a couple had dryers. Still hung the clothes out on the lines to dry. It looked like a mile of clothes hanging on the poles between the yards, those days."

"Yesterdays, Jimmy," she says.

My eyes start to get a little teary. I remember how my mother—God rest her soul—would ask me to help her fold the sheets and the smell of them had been a smell like the smell of Mary's hair underneath my chin and all of a sudden I'm thinking of the baby growing inside her and that's when I can't explain it anymore, this feeling that makes me want to cry.

So I stand up and I says, "I'll give the stew a stir."

"Mr. Delvin called about an hour ago," Mary says. "He wants you to give him a call."

14

WHEN I CALL DELVIN, HE TELLS ME HE'D AP-
preciate a visit the following morning about ten o'clock,
a little report maybe on how I was settling into the
responsibility he'd had for more than forty years. He
makes it sound like now that he's handed me the job
of ward leader on a silver platter I got no more use for
him. That's the way an old politician's mind works,
always trying to keep you off balance, taking a little
edge.

The next day I present myself on the front doorstep of
his grand old house over to Bridgeport in the Eleventh.

A lot of people think a ward leader has to live in the
ward he's supposed to be the leader of, but that ain't
the case. A committeeman can live anywhere as long
as it's inside the city limits of Chicago. And there's
even been a couple of times when a warlord decided to
move out to the suburbs, beyond greater Chicago, and
still ran his ward.

If living in the ward had been a requirement, Delvin
would've give up his position in the Twenty-seventh

long ago because he loves Bridgeport as much as Hizzoner—the late Richard J. Daley—used to do. In fact
they lived about a block away and around a corner from
each other for years.

I'm thinking about this when Mrs. Thimble, Delvin's
housekeeper, opens the door and says, "Won't you be
coming in, Mr. Flannery?"

For a second there I glance over my shoulder to see
if somebody with my name happened to walk up behind
me, because Mrs. Thimble ain't never shown me so
much courtesy since I got her this job after Delvin's old
housekeeper, Mrs. Banjo, passed away and the priest
that Mrs. Thimble kept house for died in an accident—
may God rest their souls.

"Huh?" I says, which should have been enough to
draw a scornful remark, but instead she says, "Please
come in. Mr. Delvin and his gentlemen friends are waiting in the parlor."

I follow her down the hallway with the fading pictures of long-dead people on the walls. She steps aside
and motions me to go on through.

"May I get you some refreshment, Mr. Flannery? Mr.
Vellitri and Mr. Dunleavy are having highballs. Mr. Delvin is having iced tea."

I glance at Delvin, who's sitting there looking like a
wise, tired old elephant, and I see a twinkle in his eye.

I'm not sure about Dunleavy but I know that Vellitri
don't drink as a rule and I doubt he's ever touched a
highball.

I'm about to say I'll have an iced tea when Delvin
pipes up like he can read my mind.

"Funny weather we're having. Deceptively warm. Iced
tea might sound refreshing but I've an idea there's a
nasty chill in the air which can only get worse as the
day goes on, so something warming might be the best
idea."

I don't hardly ever drink either, but I don't think Mrs. Thimble knows that, so I says I'll have a highball and she goes to fetch it.

"I think you know everybody," Delvin says, making a gesture with his hand.

Which is an understatement if I ever heard one.

I know Wally Dunleavy, the superintendent of Streets and Sanitation, almost as long as I know my old Chinaman, Chips Delvin. He's a man I've gone to many a time because he knows more about the layout of the city than any man alive.

Vito Vellitri, the warlord of the Twenty-fifth, I've also known a long time. We've locked horns and tangled tails a half a dozen times over this and that.

I always used to think that Vellitri looked like a Vatican monsignor, now I think he looks like a cardinal, the way he sits there in one of Delvin's overstuffed chairs, his body very straight but relaxed, his hands lightly holding onto the arms of the chair, showing his rings.

Usually I'm coming to him because I've been ordered to or because he's sent a couple of his aides, these two panthers, Ginger and Finks, to get me. For a second I wonder how come I didn't see them two waiting outside within earshot in case they was needed, but they're good at making themselves scarce when they want to, so I know they're around somewhere.

I shake hands with Dunleavy first. It's like grabbing a handful of bird bones. I'm afraid if I squeeze too hard, they'll splinter in my hand. He feels how easy I'm taking his hand and he gives me a grip like old men'll do, proving to one and all that they got plenty of strength and vinegar left.

"How's your father?" he asks.

"He's fine, Mr. Dunleavy. Holding up."

"Holding up what?" he asks me, grinning to let me know he's making a joke.

"His end," I says.

"So, that's good. As long as you got the strength to hold up your end, things ain't all bad."

Next I go over and shake hands with Vellitri.

"This is a real pleasure, Mr. Vellitri," I says.

"How's that, Flannery?" he asks, knowing what I said can be taken more ways than one.

"Well, usually a couple of your dogs come and drag me away from whatever I'm doing, just so you can read me the riot act and ask me what I'm doing in your ward."

"You got to admit I've got that right. You've poked around in my ward a lot. Listen, Flannery, I know we got a history . . ."

We had a history all right. He tried to chase me out of his ward when I was looking into the death by bombing of this young prostitute who was killed in my ward. The two homosexuals what was found beaten to death in the Paradise Baths where Baby, the gorilla, was being housed when the heating system in her enclosure at the zoo busted down one hard winter, turned out to have been killed in a club called the Canals of Venice. A club owned by Vellitri. Which is not to say it turns out he had anything to do with it. And when I looked into Goldie Hanrahan's life after she died the way she did, Vellitri figured in it.

That happened not long ago. It was the first time he treated me nicely, even offering me a brandy and having one of his boys serve me an expresso. Also he gives my dog, Alfie, a drink of water and some hamburger.

That time I don't see him as a clever politician with strongly rumored connections to the Mafia, I see him as an old man with an ulcer trying to protect the reputation and memory of a woman who was once a young girl who came to him for advice.

"We got a history," he says, "but times are changing,

the years pass, and it's time for us to greet each other as equals."

"Well, if you mean that, Mr. Vellitri, then it really is a pleasure to meet you today."

"I mean it, Jimmy," he says.

When I go to shake Delvin's hand, Mrs. Thimble comes in with my drink at just that second, so I take it from the tray and put it in my left hand so I can shake, and while my back's to her Delvin does a little thing and the first thing I know I'm holding what's left of his iced tea and he's got my rye and ginger ale. It's as neat as a magician's card trick.

"I was meaning to come see you as soon as I got things figured out, Mr. Delvin," I says.

"You can be in this business a hundred years and never get things figured out, lad," Delvin says. "All you can do is take one step at a time and protect your ass with both hands. You blot your copybook too many times and then you find out you can't do anybody any good at all, least of all yourself. So have a chair."

I sit down and take a sip from his glass. What's in the bottom is bitter and I realize he's already changed glasses with one of the other guests—maybe both of them—and he's handed me the remains of a highball so he can get a fresh full one.

I put the glass down and lean back in the chair waiting to see what's what, this little gathering of old men facing me. I feel a little older myself and I know it's because they're treating me differently, with a kind of respect that's heavier and more solemn somehow than they used to treat me before. I know it ain't me that's changed, it's them—the way they feel toward me now that I'm sort of on a par with them.

"So, how you settling in, Jimmy?" Dunleavy asks.

"Pretty good."

"It ain't an easy job."

"Oh, I know that. Don't I know that?"

"I envy you," he says.

"How's that, Mr. Dunleavy?"

"I envy the place you're at, the first rung of the ladder on the climb to success."

"Uh, Mr. Dunleavy," I says, "I got no ambitions for higher office or—"

"You remind me of myself when I was your age," he goes on like he didn't hear a word I said. "I was just elected committeeman of the Thirty-first—this was before it went Hispanic—back when Thomas P. Keane— God rest his soul—was alderman. I was still the ward leader when he died in '45 and his son Thomas E.— then a state senator—took over his seat on the council, a Chicago alderman always having been a more important and influential man than a state senator any day of the week."

"Wally . . ." Delvin says, trying to stem the tide, but Dunleavy's in full flood already and not about to be shunted off his theme or shut up before he's told us everything, flushing out the memories piled up in him for lack of telling, clogging up his heart.

"It was upon my advice," Dunleavy says, "that young Keane, Jacob Arvey from the Twenty-fourth, Al Horan from the Twenty-ninth, Joe Gill from the Forty-sixth and Dawson from the Second combined to oust Kennelly and run Dick Daley for mayor. Not a good many know that. Not long after . . ."

He went on like that, telling us the entire history of Chicago politics and his part in them, Vellitri sitting there very politely, scarcely moving, showing respect to a man of age and honors, while Delvin signals me to do something to shut the old man up, but I can't think what.

The light in the room starts growing dim. Vellitri coughs and stirs and finally gets to his feet.

Delvin struggles to his feet like a huge land turtle what's been thrown on its back and has to thrash around a lot to get back on its feet.

I stand up, too, but Dunleavy just goes on, his eyes and thoughts fifty years in the past.

Vellitri reaches for my hand and murmurs something about how we'll have another chance to talk sometime soon. With the other hand he hands me one of his cards.

"This is my private number," he says. "Any time you need my help, all you got to do is call."

"Likewise," I says. "I mean, I ain't got a private number, but I'm in the book and I'm available any time."

"Thank you," he says in this grand manner, and then Delvin's shambling over to the entry hall with Vellitri, two old men, the one a careful dresser, a dignified dandy, the other wearing his suit like it was the skin of an elephant, leaving me standing there thinking how Vellitri and Delvin and Dunleavy accept me now. These old men who'd once been powers in the city and were still holding on to what they had left.

I sit down and listen as Dunleavy drones on for a bit, then slows down and finally stops talking. Delvin comes back and stands there as though ready to see me and Dunleavy out, the meeting—such as it was—having come to an end.

"He put hisself to sleep," I says.

"He just stopped by. He wasn't invited," Delvin says.

"How about Vellitri?"

"He asks to have a little talk with me. He says he has an interest in something that happened in my ward and wants to show me the courtesy of informing me about it before going ahead and having a look around."

"What's that?"

"I tell him I'm not the man to ask permission. I tell him the Twenty-seventh ain't my ward any more. I tell him it's your ward and if he has anything to discuss, you should be the one to talk to. So I thought a meeting here would be all right with you, because I thought it'd make Vito more comfortable meeting in a place he's met in a thousand times before."

"But he never said what it was?"

"Dunleavy stops by before he mentions it. Dunleavy wasn't invited but he stops by all the time lately. They're finally taking Streets and Sanitation away from him, you know that?"

"I didn't know."

"Well, hell, he's too old for that kind of job. I mean he's eighty-something. I don't know exactly. At least it's for sure that he's too old," Delvin says, and blinks at me like some elephant that's too old for doing any more tricks hisself. "They're going to take Sewers away from me, too."

"Well, I don't think they're exactly going to take it away from you," I says. "It's more like they're going to want you to take a well-earned rest, put down the load."

"Considering the stuff we deal with, you got to watch out with remarks like that," Delvin says, grinning from ear to ear.

"I get your meaning," I says.

"It's going to happen any day now. I've been putting in the word, Jim, but I don't think it's going to do any good."

"What's that?" I says, but I already know what he's talking about.

"You taking over my office. The mayor wants a graduate sanitary engineer in the job."

"I can understand that."

"I can get you moved over to Public Works, the same job grade you got now. Get you a supervisor's job in Construction Services."

"They design and build new bridges, subways, streets, and parking lots, don't they?"

"They also do waterworks and sewers. It'll get you up out of the pipes. White collar job."

"I don't know if I'd be comfortable sitting behind a strange desk in a strange office wearing a suit and tie."

"Well, I can understand that. But if you stay on in Sewers, I can't promise you a future."

"Well, I got a future. I'm the committeeman of the Twenty-seventh, thanks to you, and my wife's going to have a baby any day now, and I like the work I been doing all these years."

"It's a pity that hands-on experience don't count for very much anymore," Delvin says, and then grins again.

15

On THE WAY HOME I'M WONDERING ABOUT
what Vellitri wanted to do in the Twenty-seventh that
makes him think he's got to inform the ward leader.
And I wonder if he don't bother bringing it up when he
finds out that he can't pay the courtesy to Delvin but
has to pay it to me because I stepped over the line into
his ward more than once and he figures he don't owe
me the courtesy just yet.

Whatever he wants to do—I'm willing to bet—it's going to have to do with Italians.

It's very hard to pin down an area in a city, what
with neighborhoods slopping over onto one another, and
voting districts being reapportioned, and police districts
overlayed on top of wards, and them being slapped down
on top of church parishes, and neighborhoods like Little
Italy moving several blocks or being cut in half like the
old section was cut in half when the campus of the
University of Illinois was built, for which they had to
knock down all the old tenements along Halstead where
a couple of generations of Italians grew up.

But I know there's still some old country Italians—
at least their kids—still living in the Twenty-
seventh.

So any business Vellitri has in my ward'll be something to do with the old-time *paesanos*—of which very
few are still alive.

Even though that don't tell me what the business
or the person he's got the business with might be, it
don't take a genius to figure out that it could very
well have to do with Mr. Porky, a man who was trying
to lose weight and carried no identification, but kept
a note from a complaining neighbor and some old lire
in his pockets. Also some magazines full of naked
ladies in his briefcase. Who probably wasn't living in
his regular neighborhood at the time of death and
who—it now looks—might've died under suspicious
circumstances.

But, I says to myself, since nobody's asking my opin-
ion in this matter, I'm going to mind my own business
for a change and butt out.

Which Mary tells me is a joke the minute I get home
and tell her about what happened over to Delvin's
house.

"If what you're telling me is right. If somebody's trying to cover up the death of this Mr. Porky or the circumstances surrounding it—if he died by misadventure
and not accidentally or by natural causes—well then,
sooner or later, you're going to worry and fret about
this person dying the way he did within your sphere of
influence—"

"My what?" I says.

"Your sphere of influence."

"I used to be a party worker with a precinct. Now I'm
a ward leader with a sphere of influence?"

"That's how it works, James," she says, having fun with me. "You are now a mover and a shaker with bigger things to come."

"About eight pounds six ounces from the look of things," I says.

"Bite your tongue."

16

For YEARS MIKE AND ME USED TO MEET FOR a kielbasa and cabbage dinner over to Dan Blatna's Sold Out Saloon in the Thirty-second over on the northwest side. It used to be Big Ed Lubelski's ward but Big Ed passed away two years ago—God rest his soul—and the Hispanics have moved in, so it's about half and half. So that's the way it goes, the neighborhoods—the whole city—changing right before our very eyes.

So that's what Mike and me used to do every Wednesday night until I started living with Mary and then got married. Now that Mary's home most of the time, except for a very few hours at the desk over to Passavant and the volunteer time she gives to the prenatal clinic at the Mary Thompson Hospital every Wednesday and Friday, Mary says I ought to start having a night out with my father like I used to do.

Which we do. One night or the other, Wednesday or Friday when Mary's working, depending.

But we don't go over to the Sold Out anymore because I'm on a diet and that kielbasa and cabbage is guaranteed to put on the pounds.

We decide to meet at a restaurant called the Green Grocer's which just opened up near the university campus. It's a vegetarian place with very good food, if you like vegetables, beans, pasta, and rice, and has these pretty college girls and nice-looking college boys waiting table.

It's a very noisy place because the kids pile in there but that's all right, Mike and me always get a table over in the corner out of the traffic. We sit there under this tree in a pot and run through the events of the last seven days, even though he's eating at our flat maybe half the nights of the week and anything I got to say he's probably already heard.

Every Wednesday he manages to get to the Green Grocer's before me and I find him sitting there drinking a beer and looking at the sweet young things the way old men look at sweet young things. Like a recovering alcoholic looks at a bottle of rare brandy or a diabetic looks at a hot fudge sundae.

When I walk in this Wednesday, I suddenly realize that this is one week during which I ain't seen much of him except the night when Delvin hands over the reins of the Twenty-seventh to me, to which Mike was invited.

"So, how's the committeeman this fine evening?" Mike says, putting on a bit of the brogue, as though we was a couple of politicians from the old days when Hinky Dink Kenna and Bathhouse John Coughlin ran the First. A little vaudeville my old man likes to put on every once in awhile.

"I'd give my left arm for some of Dan Blatna's sausage," I says.

"We can always hop a cab," he says, patting his own stomach which is, I notice, flatter than mine, what with all the jogging he's been doing lately.

"I notice you've been knocking yourself out getting

into shape," I says. "You going to enter the Senior Olympics or you got a lady you're trying to impress?"

"Can't a man want to keep in shape for his own sake?" he says, a little testy there, and I got a feeling I hit something on the nose.

"Well, I was just wondering were you seeing somebody because I notice you ain't been around for supper since I can't remember when and you even canceled us out last Wednesday night."

"Well, I saw you Saturday when Delvin gave you the crown. How's it fit?"

"Even so, it ain't like you to miss a Wednesday night or miss coming over for supper for more than a week."

"All right—you got to know—I've been walking out with someone."

"Anyone I know?"

"Yes, somebody you know."

"Oh, yeah? Who?"

The waitress comes over and I order a fruit salad. Mike orders a double dish of pasta with sauteed vegetables and won't say anymore about his lady friend until the food comes. Then he piles on the grated Parmesan cheese and starts right in eating without another word.

"So, tell me what's new," he says, when he's finished with his pasta and he's starting on his second beer.

"You tell me about this lady friend and then I'll tell you what's new," I says. "You say I know her?"

"For God's sake, Jimmy, you're like a goddam junkyard dog. Once you get your teeth into something you just won't let it go. Of course you know who the woman is."

Then it hits me, the way they pick at each other all the time, making sarcastic remarks about one another when they ain't in each other's company and making the same kind of cracks when they are. They both like to argue politics, Aunt Sada being socialist and Mike being old-line regular organization Democrat. They both like to eat, though Aunt Sada makes as big an effort to stay trim as my old man's been doing lately. They both like the Cubs. I mean what we've got here is a couple of dream clients for some matchmaker.

"Aunt Sada," I says.

He cuts me a look like he ain't saying yes and he ain't saying no and takes a swallow of beer like that's the end of the conversation. He's done his part, now it's time for me to do mine and answer his opening question, put the conversation back on me where he thinks it belongs.

"So?" he says. "How's it swinging?"

"Pretty good. I had my first open house over to the office Janet's lending me every Monday night. It's very different sitting there having people coming to you with their problems than you going out, sticking your foot up on somebody's porch and listening to their gripes."

"Well, I don't suppose you get to do that much nowadays anyways," he says. "Television keeps everybody inside and off the porches even on nice nights. That and air conditioning, if people can afford it. Hot nights years ago, everybody sat out on the porches and stoops."

"You still see a little of it. People are getting a little tired of the tube—"

"Same old thing."

"—I think. They're coming out on the porches and stoops on warm nights again."

"But not like it was years ago."

"Oh, no, not like that."

"But I understand what you're saying," Mike says. "You walk around, chew the fat, something comes up, it don't look like such a big deal. You can do somebody a favor, you do them the favor. Nowadays, in your position, you can't cover the whole ward, you got to have a base. Someplace people can come to."

"That's right. And then what you got is you got people afraid to come down. It starts to look official, you know what I mean? They feel like they're back to square one, trying to find a way into the system. Coming to see you is like taking the first step into the maze."

"Efficiency," Mike says.

"What?"

"Efficiency. It kills the common touch every time. Give people a number and make them wait in line and you might as well tattoo the goddam number on their forehead, make them just another cog in the machine."

"Also, the problems they bring to me ain't getting the water turned on if the old man's out of work or seeing to it some mother with kids gets a second-hand fridge so she can keep the milk—when she's got milk—from going sour. The problems are more complicated."

"Like what?"

"Like it looks like half the girls in the ward between the ages of fourteen and twenty-four are pregnant and practically none of them are under a doctor's care."

"They can't afford it," Mike says.

"That's right. They ain't got the money and they don't know how to tap into the available services, and when they try to tap into the available services, they find out there ain't enough to go around. Like the federal government's already taken the funding away from a lot of family planning outfits that were giving prenatal care because they were afraid they'd be teaching contraception, passing out the pill or advising these young girls to have abortions. Now the state's talking about laying down some tough guidelines that'll end up closing down some more unless their administrators learn how to lie and walk the wire."

"These big government types can be very stupid sometimes," Mike says.

"So that's part of what I'm wondering about. Here I

take one step up the ladder—I ain't even got any ambitions for elective office—and already I'm beginning to feel that I'm part of the bureaucracy. Part of the problem instead of part of the solution."

"Well, you ain't. The way you got to look at it is this. When you was a precinct captain, you had certain tools in your hands to get a job done. You had your contacts with people in different departments. You had your bank account of favors owed and favors due. You had some knowledge about how things work. And you had Delvin to go to if you needed a little extra clout."

"Which he was very stingy about giving."

"Which could've also been a compliment. He figured you could always work things out on your own. Which you did and which you're going to keep on doing. Except. Except now you got the power Delvin had. You're going to sit down with the other seventy-nine ward leaders from time to time. You're going to break bread with all the aldermen and the heads of departments. Ray Carrigan's not going to be the county chairman of the Democratic Party, he's going to be a colleague. So what you got to do is you got to learn how to let them come to you."

"I miss just walking around chewing the fat already."

"That's the price you got to pay. So, you'll see, there's going to be other rewards. I'll bet you already notice that people treat you different."

"That's right," I says.

"That's because they always liked you, Jimmy, even respected you, but now they got their eye on you because they don't know how far you might decide to climb."

"I told you, I ain't got any ambitions."

"Sometimes that ain't the gas that runs the engine. Sometimes people hand you a job and you got to take it because you'll end up thinking less of yourself if you don't."

Mike has another beer and I have a cup of herb tea which tastes like somebody boiled a sock in it and then I ask for the check.

"You find out who that buster was, dropped dead in front of you?" he asks.

"How do you know I'm looking?"

"Hey, you got friends. You think I ain't got friends?"

"They put a red cover on his file down at the morgue."

"Who wants it confidential?"

"I got a notion but I ain't got a clue. You got any ideas?"

"Well, first you'll have to tell me what you already got."

So I run it down for him. The old photographs taken in Naples, Italy, years ago, the silver coins—collector's pieces—adding up to thirty lire, the girlie magazines, the lack of identification and no known address.

I tell him about how Princess Grace and Shimmy Dugan never got the man's name and how he always paid by cash. How we search the man's locker and find the note from the angry neighbor who's trying to get some sleep. How I think the man's not only hiding out but trying to change his appearance.

I also tell him about being asked over to Delvin's because Vellitri wanted to inform the ward leader of the Twenty-seventh—which was now me—about things he intended to do in the ward, but nothing was finally said because Dunleavy had dropped by uninvited and Vellitri couldn't sit around any more.

"That's your notion about who put the red cover on this dead man's file at the morgue?"

"That's right. I think the man could've been Italian.

Anything to do with Italians you got to figure Vellitri knows about it."

"What I'd do is," Mike says, "number one, I'd talk to some of the other people taking the exercise classes. See if they know anything about this man that'll give you a rock to stand on."

I already had that in the back of my mind if I decided to pursue this thing any further but I let him go on without saying anything.

"Second, I'd get me some copies of them photographs and blow them up in case you decide to send your people around asking door to door."

"What people?" I says.

"Your precinct captains. You got an organization at your beck and call, you want to use it. You don't have to be a lone wolf anymore."

"Who's going to recognize anybody photographed sixty, seventy years ago?"

"You never know. I see a picture of somebody taken when they was young, I think I'd recognize them. It's a shot. Also a picture of the dead man. You got a picture of the dead man?"

I go into my pocket and bring out the picture taken at the Paradise Health Club.

Mike stares at it a minute, then he frowns, then he smiles. "You know who this looks like?"

"Who's it look like?"

"I don't mean really. I mean who it reminds me of."

"Who?" I asks, even though I got a good idea what he's going to say.

"You. You know the picture your mother took of you when you was four or five? You were fat just the way this guy is. The way he's standing with his knees bent in like that. That's the way fat kids stand. You see the resemblance?"

"I noticed it."

He hands the photo back to me.

"He could maybe be Hungarian," he says.

"Hungarian?"

"Well, Hungarians are dark, you know what I mean?"

"I think he's Italian."

"So, you think he's Italian, why don't you go have a real talk with Vito Vellitri and ask him straight out if what it was he wanted to talk to Delvin about that he didn't talk to you about, had anything to do with this man."

"I got a feeling he won't tell me. I got a feeling if he wanted to tell me, he would've told me, and Dunleavy running off at the mouth wouldn't't've stopped him."

"He tells you, he don't tell you, makes no difference. You've got to demand his respect."

"Okay. Maybe that's what I'll do. But first I think I push a button here and there first. If Vellitri freezes me out, I'd like to have something more to stick under his nose than a bunch of questions."

"What kind of buttons? Whose buttons?"

"I could lean on Eddie Fergusen down to the morgue, tell him to let me have a look at the red-cover file," I says.

"I wouldn't do that," Mike says. "You can't do things like that anymore. A little person can cut corners, something like that. A bigger person's got to watch out for protocol and principle because he's forging the relationships he's going to need in future. If you tried an end run on somebody like Dr. Hackman before, he probably would've brushed it off—even think it was funny—but you try the same thing now, he'll only get mad and he won't forget. No. It comes around you got to know what's in that file, you go to Hackman and you trade him favors."

The waitress comes with the check and I lay down the necessary cash.

"Also, you got to get yourself a credit card, Jimmy," my old man says. "You got to start keeping records for your income tax."

While we're walking to the door he says, "Oh, by the way, that other thing—"

"What other thing?"

"We'll keep it quiet, will we?"

"Keep what quiet?"

"My interest in a certain relative. Not even a word to Mary, if you'll do me the courtesy." He's talking with a brogue again. "And, for heaven's sake, boy, you've got to learn to keep more than one thing in your mind at a time."

17

THE NEXT DAY I GO DOWN TO THE POLICE property room at the Twelfth District station. There's a new man behind the counter. A Hispanic. I know better than to ask where the other cop—the one I know—is, because if you do that instead of acting like you're really happy to be having the chance to make a new acquaintance, then you take something away from the person in front of you. It's always better to ask for what you want and let them tell you they can't help you and then you ask them to help you get to the right place or person, which means they end up giving you a hand after all. Which makes them feel good. Which means they got your marker. Which means they'll remember you the next time you bump into one another.

So I says, "Good morning. My name's Jimmy Flannery. Maybe you're the man what can help me"—I catch his name off his ID—"Officer Cintron."

"I can't help you unless you tell me what it is you want," he says.

"You're my kind of man," I says. "No fooling around. Get right to the point."

99

"So do it and never mind the marmalade."

"Marmalade?"

"Most people just spread a little butter but you're all sweetness and light, ain't you? You got to go the extra mile. So you went the extra mile and I feel all gooey. So what is it?"

This man has had a bad night or the wife had a fight with him this morning or his dog peed in his shoe. Something.

"Some things would've been brought in about two weeks ago. The Saturday afternoon before last to be exact. I wonder if I could have a look."

"You a lawyer?"

"Well, what I—"

"Maybe you're a cop."

"I'm trying to tell you—"

"How about you're the owner of this property."

"—that I'm not a lawyer, a cop, the owner, or the next of kin. I'm somebody who was there when this man dropped dead and I saw some of the deceased man's belongings and I wanted another look."

"Because why?"

"Because I got an interest."

"I can see that you got an interest, but have you got a right? That's the question, ain't it?"

"I could go upstairs and see Captain Pescaro—"

"Good suggestion," he says, starting to turn away.

"—but I don't see no reason to bother Pescaro for a little thing like this."

"While you're seeing the captain, ask him to give you a pass. You should be wearing a pass on your pocket so some cop don't wonder who you are, maybe put you in the holding cell."

"Everybody knows me here. There'd be no sense me getting a pass every time I walked into the station."

"Well, I don't know you, do I?"

"I told you, I'm Jimmy Flannery."

"And who's Jimmy Flannery?"

"I'm the committeeman of the Twenty-seventh Ward."

"Oh," he says, in this different tone of voice, like I just said a magic word. "You the man holds open house over to Alderman Canarias's storefront Monday nights?"

"Well, I did last Monday night and I expect I'll be doing it every Monday night."

"I live in Mrs. Quintana's neighborhood."

"That's the old lady whose great-granddaughter's—"

"Rosa."

"—going to have a baby pretty soon?"

"That's right. Well, Rosa's my second cousin through marriage. I don't see the girl all that much but my wife keeps in touch and she wants to thank you for what you're doing for her cousin."

"I ain't doing very much. I give her an address where she can go and get some of the information and care she should've been getting the last four or five months."

"I understand that. It's very hard getting these people to look for help. They ain't got any education. They don't know how to ask."

"What people are we talking about, here? She's your family. You or your wife should've taken her by the hand, if you had to."

"I know, I know. It's very hard to keep up with everything, you know what I mean? And when you've got a big family like we got, you sort of leave it up to somebody else to do what's got to be done."

"And sometimes nobody does it."

"That's right. So, what was it you wanted?"

Just then Benedetto comes into the room and steps up beside me at the counter.

"Hey, Flannery," he says. "How's it going?"

"Well, you know," I says, "up and down and 'round and 'round. You?"

"Sixes and sevens," he says.

While I'm wondering about these stupid things we say, which are the rituals of this particular society, he asks me what I'm in the property room for.

"I want to look at Mr. Porky's stuff, if that's all right."

"That's up to the property officer," Benedetto says.

"Coming right up," Cintron says.

When he leaves the counter, Benedetto raises his eyebrows and says, "How come Cintron's so accommodating? He ain't even that pleasant to me when I ask him to get me something. You old friends?"

"We just now met," I says. "But I know a relative of his."

"Happy coincidence," Benedetto says.

"I suppose you could call it a lucky chance," I says, "but actually it's not very surprising to me. You walk around meeting people as many years as you and me been meeting people, it's really no surprise when you got a connection with practically everybody you meet, even for the first time."

"Well, I guess you're right about some of that. I suppose I'd know somebody who knew somebody who knew every crook and con man in the district."

"There you go," I says.

Cintron comes back with the usual manila envelope. "Didn't carry much, did he?" he asks as he dumps the contents out on the counter.

I look over the note and the photos again, but I don't see nothing I didn't see before.

"What kind of dog is that?" Cintron asks.

"Looks like some kind of miniature greyhound," I says.

"Maybe a whippet?" Cintron says.

"That's an Italian greyhound," Benedetto says.

I look at him like he's making a little joke.

"No, no, I ain't kidding," he says. "That's what it is. I know something about dogs and that ain't a whippet and it ain't a miniature English, it's an Italian. I got an uncle used to raise them for show. You don't see them around very much anymore."

"So, I wonder would it be all right if I got some copies of the note and the photographs," I asks, letting the question sort of land between them so I wouldn't be challenging anybody's authority or putting anybody on the spot.

"I don't see that could do any harm," Benedetto says. "You do what you want to do, Cintron. It's your shop."

Cintron picks up the two pages of the note and the photos.

"One of each?" he asks.

"That'd be just fine," I says.

Benedetto's looking through the magazines. I notice the cover price is seven and a half bucks each.

"I could never figure how come," Benedetto says.

"How come what?"

"How come some buster who wants to look at tits and crotches don't buy *Playboy, Penthouse, Hustler*, even? That gets about as graphic and gynecological as anybody could want. All of it hanging out there in living color. Really stop-your-heart beautiful women. Pictures taken by the best photographers. Besides, you get pages of jokes and articles in case you want to read yourself to sleep. And cheaper than these skinny magazines with mostly black and white photos taken in some motel, somebody's single flat. Lousy lighting. Average looking broads."

"That's it," I says.

"What's what?"

"The cheap motel, somebody's bedroom, women what wouldn't win any contests, grainy black and whites—"

"Yeah, yeah?"

"Well, that's it. A man looks at those beautiful dreams in the colored slicks, it's very hard for him to convince himself he'd have a chance with women like that." I tapped the page in the magazine he was looking at and another picture in the one he'd left opened up on the counter. "A man could imagine meeting a woman who looks like this, the waitress in the coffee shop, the girl behind the counter in the drug store, maybe the next door neighbor even. He can get a fantasy going. You understand what I mean?"

"You got a thought there. This one could be my wife's cousin's sister-in-law," he says, turning the magazine he's got in his hand so I can have a look.

"Hey," I says.

"You know her?" he asks.

"This girl's the same one in the magazine I looked at the other day," I says, "but it ain't the same magazine."

We go through the rest of them—there's five all together—and the same girl shows up in every one of them, which is more than just coincidence.

I check the covers. Every one's got a different title and a different month spread over about a year. I check the mastheads. They're all made by the same publisher over in Cicero and edited by the same editor, a guy by the name of Melvin Szpur.

When Cintron comes back with my copies, I ask him if he'd mind copying the pages in a few of the magazines which I already marked with little pieces of paper I tore from my notebook. He gives me the old one-eye but says okay. Benedetto grins. "She look like the girl next door?" Benedetto says, pulling my leg.

"I'm a married man, soon to be a father," I says.

"It don't cost anything to look," he says. "Got to go."

I've got the copies of the photographs in my hands and I'm reading the note when Cintron comes back with the copies of the magazine pictures in a clean manila envelope.

"Here, let me put them others in here so they won't get dirty," he says, so I hand them over and he puts everything in the envelope and hands it to me.

I'm just about to walk out the door when Pescaro comes walking in.

"Well, hello there, Jimmy. You come to see me?"

"No, I just stopped by. Wondered if you knew anything more about Mr. Porky."

"That reminds me, Jimmy," he says, "you can forget about asking your people to go around looking for that person."

"You found out who he is?"

"Well, not exactly, but we're following certain leads which could take us into somewhat sensitive places and your efforts, no matter how well-intentioned, could muddy the water, maybe scare people off."

"What you're saying is somebody wants Mr. Porky's identity kept quiet."

Pescaro's eyes go hard on me. Being the kindly cop ain't his best role. "Look here, Flannery, I had no right to ask for your cooperation—a civilian's cooperation— in the first place. So, now I'm telling you not to bother. You understand?"

"Didn't I just say I understood?"

"It happens all the time, Flannery. Somebody dies and the family don't want a lot of publicity."

"You telling me Mr. Porky was somebody famous?"

"I'm telling you I ain't gonna explain any more. What's that you got there?"

He reaches out and tugs at the manila envelope which I got tucked under my arm.

"Private property," I says.

"Like hell," he says, yanking it away. "This is a police

property room envelope. I got a right to examine the contents."

I don't know if he's got the right, he ain't got the right, but I do know it ain't something I can argue about.

He fans out the copies of the girlie photos.

"For God's sake, Flannery, you're too old for this sort of thing. I'll just keep them before they fall into your wife's hands."

He stares at me as though waiting for me to say something, but I got nothing to say.

18

I FIND THE PUBLISHING HOUSE—IF YOU WANT to call it that—on a road lined with small empty factories and warehouses. It's not the kind of neighborhood I'd want to go walking around in at night alone or even with somebody very big. I'm not even all that comfortable walking around in the daytime.

I don't find it right off the bat. Then I figure out that the way the numbers work, the place I'm looking for is on the side of this long building what looks like half an airplane hangar.

It's all chopped up into smaller spaces, judging by the number of doors in the wall, most likely for businesses like small-time plumbing and tile contractors that ain't got much use for a lot of space since they don't keep a lot of inventory on hand.

Canterbury Publishing is between a company that wholesales roofing supplies and another one that sells surgical supports for hernias and problems like that.

Inside Canterbury it ain't no cathedral. There's a plywood counter on the right side of the reception room.

The wall behind it is practically papered with the centerfolds of the magazines they publish, all pasted up on top of one another so you get parts of some bodies growing out of some very funny places on other bodies.

There's the biggest old rolltop desk I ever seen in my life sitting there with a telephone on the chair in front of it. It's closed and I get the feeling from the quiet in the room and on the other side of the plywood partition that nobody's at home.

I walk around the end of the counter and peek inside the other room which is about the same size as the one with the desk. One wall is stacked up with baled magazines and there's a long trestle table in the middle of the room with a bunch of loose magazines scattered around, and an old army cot shoved up against the opposite wall. Nobody home, just like I thought.

There's two other doors at the back of the room and I figure one leads back outside and the other leads to a toilet.

"Hello!" I says, just to make sure.

When I get no answer, I take a couple of steps closer to the back of the room and say it again.

When that don't get me nothing, I yell, "Hey, anybody in there?"

"In where?" a voice says at my back and I spin around to face this character with mussed-up ginger-colored hair and a pointy nose with little round specs sitting on the end of it.

It don't take a genius to see that I woke him up. He gives me a yawn and a view of his gold caps just to pin it down. I can see over his shoulder that the rolltop is up on the desk.

"Was you sleeping in the desk?" I asks.

"I was *resting* in the desk," he says, like I was insulting him. "When I sleep, I sleep on that cot over there."

"Why was you resting in your desk?" I asks.

"Can you think of a better place? It's warm, it's cozy, if you like your own smell it offers a familiar atmosphere and it's quiet. Except when strangers come in and shout at the toilet door," he adds.

"My name's Jimmy Flannery," I says. "So now we ain't total strangers anymore."

He grins at me.

"Well, at least we're halfway there," I says. "Would you happen to be Melvin Szpur?"

"I would happen to be."

"Is that Polish?"

"Bohemian," he says.

He's still grinning at me when he says that if I want to take a magazine and sit down, he'll go back to the rolltop and make us both a cup of cocoa. Instant.

I go sit on a stack of magazines, after picking up a copy of the newest one I saw at the police property room off the table.

In a couple of minutes he comes back with two mugs of cocoa, hands me one, sits down on another stack of magazines, and smiles at me.

"Are you a fan?" he says.

"A what?"

"Are you one of our constant readers?"

"Well, I'll tell you—"

"If you're looking for the name and address of one of our models, you're out of luck."

"I wanted to know who this ..." Whatever I was going to say I don't say because what he said caught up with me before I could say it.

He looks at me from over the top of his glasses.

"Ah ha," he says. "Can I read minds or can I read minds? Of course, on the other hand, it's very rare for anybody to stop by here for any other reason unless it's a bill collector."

"How do you know I ain't a bill collector?"

"Because you don't look like a bill collector."

"What does a bill collector look like?"

"Can I read minds or can I read minds?" he says again.

I get the feeling we could get caught in a circle and go on forever or at least until the cocoa gets cold, so I takes a swallow and asks, "Do you get many people stopping by asking for names and addresses?"

"Now and then."

"What do they want?"

"Two things in the main," he says. "Either they want to meet one of the models because they've fallen desperately in love with her picture or they believe they've chanced upon a picture of a lost wife, sister, or daughter. One quest is as sad as the other."

"Do you ever help somebody out with a name or an address?"

"Why should I? I could be dealing with a vengeful relative or a nut, either one of whom might do the girl some harm."

"Or they might be trying to help her."

"Should I take the chance?"

"Can you read minds or can you read minds?" I says.

"Put my foot in my own mouth, didn't I?" he says.

"If you think you can, I'd like you to look me over real good and tell me if you think I'm out to hurt anybody."

He stares at me for a long time. I almost get the feeling he actually can get inside my head and see what's there.

"I think you're a man who can be taken at his word."

"I'm not out to hurt this woman in any way," I says. I show him the spread on the girl who appears in so many of his magazines. He glances at it for only a second, then looks at me and shakes his head.

"Yes," he says. "There's something haunting in that girl's face, isn't there?"

"So, do you know who she is?"

He shakes his head again, but he hesitates a flick too long, an honest man making up his mind to lie.

"You never met her? She never come in here?" I says.

"Never." Lying don't come easy to him. His face is coloring up.

"Maybe the publisher or one of your other employees might've been here when she come in?" I went on.

"You're looking at the entire organization. I'm publisher, editor, distributor, and secretary. Not a lot of text, you've noticed, so I know you won't be surprised when I tell you I'm the entire writing staff as well."

"You take the pictures, too?"

"Some, not all. I buy from a half a dozen photographers around town. I even buy a few from agencies as far away as New York, New Orleans, and Los Angeles. The skin trade is a universal trade and a lot of people live by it, one way or another."

"You buy these from elsewhere? You know the photographer?"

He turned his head away and for a second there it looks like he's going to start crying, but he shakes his head and takes a swallow of his cocoa, and then he looks me straight in the eye.

"You're the photographer what took these pictures," I says.

"You read minds, too?" he says. "What else do you think you can tell me?"

"You was in love with her."

"Maybe I was. Are you in love with her? Do you know her? Does she belong to you?"

"No. To all of it."

"Too bad. I think she's lost. It would be nice if somebody would find her."

"That's what I'm trying to do."

"Why?"

"Because a man died and when we looked through his things we found a half a dozen of your magazines. Different ones, except this girl's pictures was in every one of them."

"A man died?"

"That's right. A man dropped dead right in front of my eyes while we was doing some exercises at a health club."

"So . . . ?" He gestured at the magazine I was still holding as though asking me what one had to do with another.

"So there's some question about how he died. No really strong suspicions but some questions, you understand what I'm saying?"

"Are you a police officer?"

"Nothing like that. A concerned citizen with a curious streak. I didn't know the man and I don't know this girl, but I'd still like to know if there was a connection."

"What did this man look like?"

I described Mr. Porky.

"A man fitting that description came in asking about Marilyn about three weeks ago."

"Marilyn?"

"That's her name. Marilyn La France. I don't believe it's her real name."

"I think you're right. You got an address on her?"

He shook his head slowly, mournfully.

"What happened?"

"I made a mistake. I was concerned when that man came asking about her. I told her about him."

"She tell you who he was, anything about him?"

"She blurted out, 'Teddy,' and made a face, but that's all she'd say. Not another word. That's the last I saw of her, except once."

"When was that?"

"Saturday before last. I went to see her where she worked."

"And where's that?"

"You know the Club Morocco over on Ogden in Cicero?"

"I can find it. What does Marilyn do there?"

"She dances."

I pick up the top magazine. "You mind I take this copy with me?"

"Go ahead, I got plenty," he says.

I carefully remove the centerfold.

"Actually this is all I want," I says. "Thanks for the picture and the cocoa."

So I left Szpur with his magazines filled with naked girls and the memory of one he obviously cared about. I had a name. Teddy. Theodore or Edward. It wasn't much.

19

A MARRIED MAN WHOSE WIFE IS ABOUT TO
have a baby shouldn't be going over to Cicero on a Saturday night. Maybe nobody should be going. Cicero and
Calumet City were the suburbs where the crime and
vice ended up back in the thirties, and even in the late
forties they said that any sheriff of Cook County who
couldn't make a million dollars off them two towns just
wasn't trying.

Things are better now, but I don't know how much
better since Cicero and Calumet City ain't part of my
territory.

The Club Morocco may have had dreams of grandeur
once upon a time but it's gone to seed. The neon sign
outside has a couple of tubes missing and the glass cases
for the posters announcing "Twenty—Count 'em—
Twenty" naked girls inside and "Total Nooooodity"
ain't been washed in a year.

As I approach, I can see that the doorman's bored out
of his head, but he brightens up when I park my car at
the curb. I tell him I may not be very long and ask him
if the car'll be all right.

"I could tell you yes, but I'd be lying," he says. "Every once in awhile the traffic wardens decide it's a tow-away zone and it'll cost you seventy-five bucks to get your car back."

"You got a parking lot?" I asks.

"Around back but it's so dark back there you might not have a car at all when you get back."

He's hustling me for a tip. It's early times and he figures if he can score a nice tip, it could be a sign of good things to come.

"But you know a place where my car'll be safe," I says.

"You give me the key. I ain't going anywhere until the club closes in case you decide to stay awhile. A traffic warden comes along and eyeballs your vehicle, I prove that it's mine. So it's okay. They don't tow it. Professional courtesy, you understand."

I hand him a five-dollar bill and he gives it the old one-eye.

"I wish it was more but my wife's about to have a baby," I says.

"My wife's already had five," he says.

"So you ever come to Chicago and need a favor, you look me up. My name's Jimmy Flannery and I'm the committeeman for the Twenty-seventh."

"You telling me the truth?" he says.

"Yes, I am," I say.

He hands me back the five. "Professional courtesy. Don't worry about your car. It'll be here when you come out. And watch yourself. Some of these girls in there is barracudas."

The minute I walk inside, the noise and smoke hits me like a pair of sledgehammers, one from either side. The smell of smoke, sweat, the glue in the water paint on the sets and walls, cheap perfume, and stale beer could choke you to death. I feel like I'm on safari making my way to the main room when a woman in an evening dress, both of which has seen better days, grabs me by the arm.

"Does your mother come from Ireland?" she says, giving my red hair a look.

"Good evening," I says.

" 'Cause there's something about you Irish," she says. "You want the bar, a table, or a booth?"

"What would you suggest?"

"Depends on what you're looking for. You want the girls to cruise you, it's better at the bar. You just want to drink, look, and clap your hands, the tables're the best. You want a cozy conversation with a girl of your choice, I'd suggest a booth."

"So, I'll take a booth."

"The cover's ten dollars for a booth."

I hand her ten dollars.

"I'll bring your first drink over," she says. "After that the waitress'll keep an eye on you. What's your poison?"

I didn't think people said "what's your poison" anymore, but I don't hang around these joints so I wouldn't really know.

"A glass of ginger ale," I says.

"You didn't bring your own flask or bottle, did you?"

"I don't drink," I says.

"Well, good for you. Ginger ale's the same price as bar whiskey."

She shows me to a booth within view of the stage where a redhead's taking her clothes off as fast as she can. She's back in a minute with my drink.

"Four bucks," the hostess says, "or you want to pay with a credit card?"

I hand her a five. "Keep the change," I says.

"I like a man who throws his money around," she says, letting me know that a buck ain't much where she comes from. "Now, the girls on stage are available for conversation between numbers. You pay for their drinks and tips are allowed, but no dates."

"Dates?"

"Making dates for after closing hours is against the law." She gives me this look which says that she's a good citizen and has spoke her piece the way the law demands but also that we're all grown-ups—ain't we?— so what I did on my own time and what the dancers did on their own time was none of her business. As long as she got her cut. "So, when you see someone that takes your fancy, all you got to do is catch my eye."

"You have a dancer by the name of Marilyn LaFrance working here?" I asks.

"Oh, boy," she says.

"What's that mean."

"You know Ms. LaFrance?"

"I've heard about her. So I'm not completely ignorant about why you said, 'Oh, boy.' "

"It means you're asking for the most popular girl ever worked in this club. She gets so many requests, I'm beginning to feel like her social secretary."

"How's her appointment book look tonight?"

"Very full. But I can always make room for an Irish redhead if you . . ."

She don't have to tell me if I what. I hand her twenty bucks, wondering how long it's going to take for me to make it up out of my lunch money for this evening's investigation.

About five minutes later, a blonde slides into the banquette alongside me, showing me a lot of leg through a slit skirt in the process.

"Howya, Red?" she says. "You wanted to see me?"

A waitress who's plenty of competition for the dancer, the way she's falling out of her blouse, ain't far behind.

"No, I want to see Marilyn LaFrance," I says.

"So, here I am," she says.

"No, you ain't."

She looks down at her front and says, "You could've fooled me."

"Yeah, but you didn't fool me."

"You want to order or something?" the waitress says.

"I could use a little champagne," the phony LaFrance says.

"That's all you drink, is it? How about a little ginger ale?"

She makes a face.

"Hey, that's what comes in the champagne bottles or maybe just some white wine needled with a carbon dioxide cartridge. So, okay, have a highball which will also be ginger ale with a little caramel coloring in it."

"Know all the tricks do you?" she says.

"I'm not trying to be a smart aleck. I'm willing to buy you a drink for your time, while you explain to me about Marilyn LaFrance."

"Betty," she says, looking up at the waitress who's standing there waiting for the train to come in, "bring me a whiskey with a ginger back."

"I'm okay, Betty," I says.

"I can see you're a slow sipper," Betty says, and high-heels it away.

"It must hurt her feet walking around in them heels all night," I says.

"It ain't as bad as showing it off up there. Last year I threw out my tailbone and I had to stay in bed for three weeks."

"I'm sorry about that."

"That's okay," she says, giving me the look. "I spend a lot of time on my back."

"Oh, my," I says.

"Does that mean I'm getting to you?" she asks, moving a little closer and getting her thigh up against mine.

"A couple of years ago, what you just said would've give me a thrill," I says.

"What happened since then? You lose something in a war?"

"I got married and my wife's having a baby."

"I know that song," she says. "She cut you off and you're feeling deprived."

The waitress comes back with the drink, which costs me another five. The dancer bangs it back while the waitress stands there, then takes a swallow of ginger ale to cut the heat.

"One more?" Betty asks.

"Don't bother, Betty," I says. "Let's take it a little slow. My girlfriend can drink the highball she just made for herself when she spit the whiskey into the ginger ale."

I smile at my companion.

"Saving your money for later?" she asks.

"What later?"

"You want to make a date for after closing time?"

"I told you I had a wife with a nice round belly waiting for me at home. I ain't feeling deprived. I'm happier then I ever been in my life and I don't mind waiting."

She gives me a long steady look and says, "Why do I believe you?"

"Because I got no reason to lie."

I take out the picture of Marilyn LaFrance—or whatever her real name might be—from my pocket and unfold it.

"I know you ain't Marilyn LaFrance because I was told this is Marilyn LaFrance."

She looks at the picture. "Harriet," she says.

"Is that her real name?"

"I don't know. Every girl who works the scene has a dozen names."

"So why did you sit down when I asked for Marilyn LaFrance?"

"I thought you knew it all. You could ask for Cleopatra and the hostess would bring over somebody. Who cares? A man's looking for a woman, I'm a woman. Any female in the joint's a woman."

"The old bait and switch."

"That's better than the old wait and bitch, ain't it?"

"So, what's your name?"

"Charlene."

"That your real name?"

"What difference does it make? You planning on adopting me?"

"All right, Charlene," I says. "You mind telling me where Marilyn LaFrance might be?"

She shrugs her powdered shoulders, which moves other parts of her anatomy and I got to admit that it's a pretty sight.

"You telling me the truth?"

"Can't you tell?"

I look at her as close as she looked at me.

"Okay," I says.

"So, now we're practically soul mates," she says.

"You think Marilyn LaFrance'll be coming back here?"

"You can bet on it."

"I got to go," I says reaching for my pocket.

She puts her hand on my arm. "Keep your money. Buy the baby a present from me."

20

THE NEXT TUESDAY NIGHT I'M AT THE HEALTH club doing the old ups and downs and side to side. There's a certain wariness among the others doing the drills, like they're remembering they could lay down for some leg lifts and never get up again or maybe that's just my imagination. Maybe it's just remembering the way P. Pig, a.k.a. Mr. Porky, looked laying there not breathing.

So the way I look at it, when you're at a certain age—which nobody knows what that age is—if you exercise too vigorously, you could drop dead. On the other hand, if you don't exercise at all and let yourself go to fat, you could drop dead.

I'm thinking all this, which is getting me nowhere in a hurry, when Princess Grace calls for an o.j. break. He gives us a little lecture on how we got to replenish the water, minerals, and vitamin C we're losing with the exercise. I think it's just his way of making a few extra bucks selling o.j. but what the hell, I'm as dry as a bone, my tongue feels like a sock and I've been waiting for the chance to talk to Lucy Frye and Mrs. Falzone first chance I get.

We belly up to the plywood drink stand Princess Grace built with his own hands. As it happens, I'm closest to Lucy Frye so I offer to buy her an o.j. which she accepts. After Princess Grace serves them up we walk over to the corner and sit down on a mat to enjoy them.

I can't help noticing again what a pretty woman Lucy Frye is and what a sensational figure she's working on there. It's not like I'm getting ideas but I'd have to think something was going wrong with me, and so would Mary for that matter, if I didn't admit that I enjoy looking at pretty women. Which don't mean that I'm about to mention Lucy Frye to Mary in the condition Mary's in because I notice women get very touchy about such comments when they ain't at their best.

"So wasn't that something?" Lucy says. "Dropping dead right next to me. I mean he touched me on the arm just before we sat down to do those leg lifts."

"Touched you on the arm?"

"Oh, he didn't mean anything funny, I'm sure. He excused himself right away. Said he just lost his balance there for a second."

"I can understand that. Sometimes even I get a little whoozy, all the up and down."

"Well, you got to be careful at your age, not to overdo it."

At my age? It hits me like a bullet between the eyes. This Lucy Frye thinks of me as an older man. I mean, does getting married and putting on a couple of pounds and getting a promotion in the party turn you into an older man? Then I says to myself it ain't those things that age you, it's the years I was spending while all those things was happening that aged me. That and responsibility.

"So he like reached out and held on to me for a second

until he got his balance," Lucy says, "and then he apologized and then we got down and did a couple sets of leg lifts and rolls and then . . ." Her face clenches up like a little fist for a second and I think she's going to cry but instead she says, "They were Teddy's last leg lifts, weren't they?"

"Teddy?"

"That's what he said his girlfriend called him. Short for Teddy Bear."

We've got a regular menagerie here, what with the Porky Pigs and Teddy Bears.

"I never heard anybody call him that around here," I says.

"I don't think he told anybody else. Once one of the other patrons asked him what he should call him and Teddy laughed and said, 'Call me anything you want as long as you don't call me late for dinner.' You remember that old joke?"

I said I did. Then I asks, "He ever tell you his last name?"

"I can't remember."

"So you just called him Teddy?"

"I suppose I did. Or maybe I figured since I wasn't his girlfriend it wouldn't be right to call a man old enough to be my grandfather, Teddy, so I didn't call him anything. It sounds a little silly, doesn't it? Teddy Bear?"

I'm sitting there trying to remember what she calls me and if she thinks she should call me Mr. Flannery because I was so much older than she was, when she jumps up—without even putting her hands on the mat—and says, "Thanks for the o.j., Jimmy."

So that's okay.

I still got a couple of minutes before we have to get back to the huffing and puffing so I take the empty cups over to the trash can, maneuvering it so I get there at the same time Mrs. Falzone's dumping her cup and a wrapper from a piece of pastry—which Princess Grace also sells but shouldn't—into the trash.

She makes a face as she wads up the waxed paper and dumps it. "So I work for two hours to burn off some calories and then I can't resist, I eat a Danish."

"It looks to me like you've been losing pretty good," I says.

"You think so, Jimmy?"

"Yes, I do, Mrs. Falzone," I says, before I realize that I'm doing to her what I was afraid Lucy Frye was going to do to me with the respectful names you use on older persons.

"Hey, I'm not your grandmother," Mrs. Falzone says. "I call you Jimmy, so you got to call me Sis. No, call me Aurelia."

"That's a pretty name."

"It ain't Italian, I can tell you. It's French. Something like that. They tell me my grandmother had a fit when my mother named me Aurelia because some character in a romantic novel was called Aurelia. So, that's all right. Hardly anybody calls me Aurelia, which would make my grandmother in heaven very happy. I never looked like an Aurelia. Forty pounds overweight ain't romantic."

"You don't look forty pounds overweight."

"You got to watch out for Irishmen and their honey-cake," she says.

"No, no, I mean it. I'm not saying you're *not* forty pounds overweight. I wouldn't know about that. I'm just saying it don't look bad on you. Some people look better with a couple of pounds on them."

"That's the second time I heard that same thing in this club," she says.

"Oh."

"Maybe that's why I come here. For the compliments."

"Somebody else said you looked fine just the way you are?"

"Oh, yes, but him saying it didn't mean anything."

"Why's that?"

"Well, he was a little childish. You know what I mean? A little silly in the head?"

"You wouldn't be talking about Teddy would you?"

"Teddy?"

"The man what dropped dead. That's what he told Lucy Frye to call him."

Mrs. Falzone laughs, like she's enjoying a big joke.

"Can you imagine that. He never liked us to call him Teddy. So, some things change."

"You knew him?"

"Well, he wasn't a friend. He was just somebody from the neighborhood."

"Where do you live, Aurelia, you don't mind my asking?"

"Over on Grand."

"Toward the lake. In the Forty-second?"

"That's right."

"And is that where he lived?"

"I don't know where he lived. I'm not talking about I saw him in the neighborhood lately. I'm talking about thirty, thirty-five years ago in the old neighborhood. St. Francis de Sales parish."

"That's down around a Hundred and Second—"

"And Avenue J." She finishes for me.

"Thirty, thirty-five years ago. How do you know it's the same man?"

"He gives me a smile the first time he sees me here. This silly grin like he knew something I didn't know. That grin should've given me the clue right there but, after all, thirty-five years had passed and he was the last person I expected to see in a health club on his own."

"Why's that?"

"He wasn't all there. I don't know if he was seriously retarded or anything like that. I mean he wasn't in the right grade for his age, but he went to school. For a while at least. Then I suppose his mother took him out. The kids used to make fun of him."

She laughs at some memory.

"Even when he was a grown man, he'd do crazy things. One summer he walked around with this clown's face he'd put on himself with his mother's lipstick and rouge. He used to like to dress up like the pictures of Al Capone. Wore a white topcoat in the summer. His mother spoiled him. Gave him practically anything he wanted. I guess she felt guilty having a child like that. I can understand that."

"So can I."

"Well, she must've done something right, otherwise he wouldn't be taking care of himself like he must've been doing. Maybe she passed away. I should've asked."

"Why didn't you?"

"Well, I've got to tell you the truth. He always gave me the creeps. That grin of his and the eyes. He'd look at you with those eyes like a little kid's and then— all of a sudden—something bad would come into them. Listen to me, will you, going on like some superstitious guinea from the old country. But I seem to remember there was some talk."

"What kind of talk?"

"About him exposing himself on the street. The girls in my family were warned to stay away from him. I don't remember exactly why, but I think it might've been that he'd tried something with some children."

"When did you remember him?"

"He came up behind me one evening and says, 'Hello, Aurelia,' which very few people ever call me, and right away I remembered. 'Hello, Theobald,' I says. That didn't please him very much. I ruined his little game.

He wanted to drive me crazy wondering where he knew me from."

"Theobald?"

"Sure. That's where he got that Teddy. Not from Theodore, from Theobald. Theobald Tramontina."

"How come you never told anybody around here about this after he dropped dead?"

"Nobody asked me," she says, giving me a look like what am I, not very bright?

"I'm sorry, Aurelia, you wouldn't have any way of knowing that we didn't have a name or address on the man. The authorities still got him on ice downtown. They ain't even been able to notify his next of kin."

She's frowning.

"He might not have been living in the old neighborhood anymore. They might not find anybody there who knew him. We're talking thirty years since I left the neighborhood. I'm sure a lot of people moved away from St. Francis de Sales parish. Even if his mother or anybody else from the Tramontina family are around, they might not talk to the police. The Tramontina family was always very good at keeping their mouths shut."

21

WHEN I GET BACK TO THE FLAT, ALFIE, WHO used to be my dog and palled around with me a lot but who's Mary's dog ever since she started staying home most of the time, is laying down in the entry hall. He gives me the old one-eye which says there's something going on which he ain't entirely happy about. I hear voices from the parlor and when I walk on through I find Mary standing there in front of a chart or something she's got pinned up on one of them portable clothes lines we used to dry the washing when it rained five or six days in a row. I'm talking about before we got a laundry room with a washer and dryer put down in the basement for the rest of the owner/tenants of the building and ourselves.

Eight young girls, Afro-Americans and Hispanics, are sitting around in a semicircle listening to every word she says.

I take a step into the room and get a look at the chart which is of a naked pregnant woman with a cutaway view of how the baby's situated inside her womb and I quick take a step right back out of there.

Mary sees me and gives me a big smile and says, "Hello, James. If you'd like to come in and meet the ladies and listen to the end of the lecture on prenatal care, you're very welcome."

The young women take a look at me—one's Mrs. Quintana's granddaughter, Rosa; another one's the girl who was with Millie Jefferson; and another one's Benedetto's maid—and give me some grins and giggles.

I've never been able to understand why women, young and old, think it's funny when a man don't choose to sit around listening to a lot of talk about morning sickness and how to use a breast pump and things like that. It's like they think men are afraid to even hear about having babies, which is not altogether true, though I admit it ain't as entertaining as talking about the chances of one of our ball teams copping a pennant.

So anyway I says, "Thank you very much and hello to all you pretty ladies, but if it's all the same to you, I think I'll go take my dog for a walk."

There's another burst of giggles as I back on out to the kitchen.

I get Alfie's leash and we leave the flat.

Walking down the street it's like old times, just Alfie and me looking over the neighborhood seeing how everybody's getting along.

Joe Pakula's standing in the doorway of the store which is in the corner of the building and he says, "Long time no see, Jimmy. I suppose your new job's keeping you busy."

"Well, no busier than I been before I had the job," I says. "Though it's true it takes me away from home more than I used to be."

"We miss you, Jimmy. The old women in the neighborhood ask about you. They ask about how come you don't wash your car every Saturday like you used to."

"Well, I should do that, but I don't seem to be able

to find the time," I says. "By the way, is there anything I can do for you?"

"I had a favor to ask. Not for me. For my cousin who just came up from South America. Well, for me, too, I suppose. Anyway, Mrs. Flannery's taking care of it. In fact my cousin's up in your flat right now."

"I saw eight girls—women—listening to my wife give them a little talk about having babies and how to take care of themselves."

"So, my cousin's one of them. It's very nice of Mrs. Flannery to open up a free family planning counseling office in your flat."

"Is that what she's doing?"

"Didn't she tell you?"

"Not yet, but I'm sure she'll get around to it."

Alfie and me go on with our walk, stopping here and there when we meet somebody we know, which ain't too often. I start thinking again about how fast things seem to be changing since I was a kid and how I'm not sure I like it very much. But like it or not, you got to just keep putting one foot in front of the other. That's the only way a person can get around the block or wherever any of us are trying to go.

"What do you think about this situation with Theobald Tramontina, also known as Mr. Porky or Mr. Pig?" I says out loud.

Alfie looks up and gives me his attention.

"What are we dealing with here? Mrs. Falzone says he could've been a little funny in the head, but what's somebody like that doing going to health clubs at night all by hisself? Which is not to say that some of these people who ain't what you'd call very bright can't do plenty of things. Going to a health club ain't the hardest thing in the world after all. On the other hand, maybe we just got a guy what likes to go around looking at ladies what are naked or half-dressed. I mean, there's the magazines. And he had something going with Marilyn LaFrance. I don't know what, but something. Maybe he wasn't just a clown missing a couple of marbles. Mrs. Falzone said there was talk about him exposing himself, fooling with children. So what the hell was he doing wandering around by hisself? You got any ideas?"

Alfie snuffles and shakes his head.

"True. We know a lot more than we knew last week but it still ain't much. It's still a puzzle what he was doing in the Twenty-seventh with no identification and no address. I mean it looks like he was hiding out. What we're not really completely sure about is how he died and if he was really the man Mrs. Falzone says he is."

By this time we're around the block. It's been a long day and I'm feeling tired. I trudge up the stairs hoping the young mothers-to-be will all be gone and nobody's come visiting in the meantime.

I don't hear any voices coming from the parlor but I peek in anyway. It's empty and so's the kitchen.

I look into the bedroom and Mary's laying on the bed. She's been letting her hair grow and now she's undone it and it's laying spread out on the pillow while she leans on one elbow reading a book. She looks at me and rolls over on her back, putting the book aside and making a place for me.

I take off my shoes and lay down next to her.

"You do any good for yourself today?" she asks.

"Well, I think I got a line on that man who died at the health club. But, I'll tell you, right now I feel like Scarlet O'Hara from that picture—"

"*Gone With the Wind.*"

"—we rented from the video store the other night. I don't want to think about it tonight. I'll think about it tomorrow."

"Not a bad idea," she says, and then she kisses me.

"I got a question," I says.

"You know a newspaper reporter by the name of B. Behan?" she asks right back.

"Yes, Billy Behan. I know him. He's a man who laughs only when somebody breaks a leg."

"He's been nosing around the clinic, asking questions, harassing patients."

"You warn him off?"

"The director tried to ask him in a nice way not to frighten our pregnant women, but he just raved on about freedom of the press and the sacred right of the public to know how their public institutions were serving them."

"I could have a talk with him," I says.

"I doubt that'd do any good. In fact it could do a lot of harm. He doesn't seem to like you. He told me so. I've got to admit it came as some surprise."

"How's that?"

"Well, even people who are against you on certain issues, still like you personally. I don't know many who don't. In any case he made it clear that if I complained to you and you complained to him, the only thing that would come of it is that he'd work that much harder to dig up some dirt on the clinic."

"He said that? He threatened that?"

"Now, don't get your Irish up," she says, like she expects me to go out there and punch him in the nose which maybe I've been known to do, but only when somebody's pushed me to the wall and there's no way out. "He's the type who'll get tired and give it up if nobody takes his challenge and fights him."

"So is that why all these young mothers about-to-be are in my parlor—which is the question which I was about to ask?"

"Which I figured," Mary says. "He spotted some literature about birth control I'd given to one of my mothers. I stopped him from questioning her and the women sitting with her in the waiting room. He went away but I know he'll be back and I don't want him bothering any of them, so for the time being at least, I'm going to have them meet here once a week."

"In our flat?" I asks, sounding a little testy. "I don't mean that to sound selfish but I'd just as soon my home didn't have people going in and out like it was the waiting room down at the Greyhound station. Also, do you think it's a very good idea for women that far along to go tramping up and down six flights of stairs?"

"I'm looking into other arrangements," she says, and kisses me again, which she knows is always an easy way to shut me up.

22

THE WEEK GOES BY WITH THIS AND THAT. I got some meter inspections down to Calumet Harbor, which ain't so far away from St. Francis de Sales, so I go down there to One Hundred Second and Avenue J, in the southeast corner of the city—which is called the East Side but which is also called South Chicago—on my lunch break. St. Francis de Sales is the East Side's oldest Catholic parish.

In the Tenth Ward, in what they call South Chicago, you got Our Lady of Guadalupe which the Mexicans built.

You've got Calumet Park, made out of the slag of steel mills.

You've got a neighborhood called Pill Hill which was once the neighborhood of a lot of doctors. Now it's one of the nicest black areas in Chicago. It's also got Helen Maybell's Soul Queen Restaurant which has got a sign on the wall what says, You may eat all you want, but you must pay for all you take.

There's Jeffrey Manor and Merrionette Manor, Slag

Valley and Hegewisch, Island Homes—which is a trailer park—and East Side, a neighborhood between the Calumet River and the Indiana state line.

Mexicans, Croats, Serbs, Poles and Italians jealously defend their turf around the Tenth.

A black man moved into an Italian neighborhood back in 1984 and they burned his garage down. So it's a place what still makes its own trouble.

By the time I get there, I feel like I ain't even in Chicago anymore.

The old St. Francis de Sales burned down back in the twenties and the new one is part of the school.

I just drive by and give it the once over, then I go back to the meters and catch a little lunch along the way.

On Sunday, which is the day when Mary and me usually sleep in, I get up early. Mary wakes up long enough to ask me where I'm going and I tell her I'm going to church and she says, "That's nice," and goes back to sleep.

I'm just in time for the eight o'clock Mass at St. Francis de Sales. The minute I walk into the vestibule—before I even get into the nave—memories come flooding back of when I was a kid and my mother—God rest her soul—used to slick me up and take me to church.

I remember when I made my First Holy Communion. I remember the white satin bow tie and white suit I had to wear which gave me the miseries.

The smell of incense is like the smell of my mother's perfume and the light coming through the stained glass windows reminds me of the twilight coming into the flat when I was small and she'd read to me from a storybook while rocking me on her lap.

The nave is maybe a tenth full of people, mostly middle-aged working men and women all dressed up in their

Sunday best and some youngsters who're probably there to see if they can meet somebody of the opposite sex.

But I'm not looking for middle-age and I ain't looking for young. I'm looking for old and there they are, the ones who came over in the twenties and thirties when they was maybe twelve, fourteen. They got work on the streets as pick and shovel laborers. They put in the time in the slaughterhouses and the steel mills and the coke yards. The girls cleaned other people's houses and worked in the five and dimes and in the factories.

They raised their families, minded their own business if they could, and grew old.

There's a whole pew filled with them, old men and women dressed in black, with white hair and hands like old wrinkled leather, the women saying their beads, the old men staring straight ahead with watery eyes.

I'm hoping that one of them can tell me what I want to know.

When the service is over, I'm one of the first out the door. A couple of people give me a look as I stand at the curb waiting for the old folks to make their way out of church, not only because I'm a stranger but—with my kisser and red hair—an Irish stranger.

An old priest comes down an alley from the rectory and takes up a place near the door, shoulder to shoulder with the younger priest who'd celebrated the Mass, and I can see that he's the old pastor of St. Francis de Sales parish and he wants to keep on shaking the hands of the faithful as long as he's got the strength.

So right there I change my plans. Instead of going up to one of these old ladies or gentlemen—who got the habit of keeping their traps shut, otherwise they wouldn't've lived so long—I'll talk to the Father.

After the congregation empties the church, I go up to him and says, "I beg your pardon, Father, but I wonder if I could have a word with you?"

"Wit' me?" he says, surprised that anybody would still want a word with him. "You shoo you don' wanna counsel wit' Father Harry, here?" He's got this old-world accent which makes his thin voice sound like water running over velvet. It's got a kind of huskiness and I figure he smokes more than he should. Probably them skinny black cigars dipped in wine.

Father Harry's giving me the old one-eye.

"No, it's you I'd like to counsel with," I says to the old priest. "My name's James Flannery and I'm the ward leader up to the Twenty-seventh."

"You're a long way from home," Father Harry says.

"In a neighborhood I ain't all that familiar with," I says. "That's why I'd like a word with the pastor."

"Do you feel up to an interview, Father Rocco?" the younger priest asks.

"I don' think this is an interview," Father Rocco says. "I think it's more like a couple of questions. Am I right?"

"That's all I'll probably have to ask. I'll be out of your hair in five minutes, maybe less."

"Will I come with you, Father?" the younger priest asks.

"No, no. You go on about your business. I know you've got a lot of paperwork to catch up on."

Father Harry gives me a look like he's telling me he's putting his most precious treasure into my hands and hurries away, his vestments making him look like a ship taking off to sea.

"The boy worries abou' me," Father Rocco says. "He makes me take twenny naps a day. So much rest is going to kill me. My arteries will sludge up. Am I right?"

"I think you could use some exercise."

"Everybody could use some exercise. So let's take a

walk over to the rectory. We'll have a little glass of wine. A little *biscótto*. A little something."

We start to walk.

"You've been here a long time, have you, Father?" I asks.

"I came righ' after the old church burned down back in '25. Can you imagine that? I was a young priest. I rebuilt the church wit' wha' we had." He stops in his tracks. I get the idea he can't walk and do too much figuring at the same time. "Sixty-five years ago. Would you believe it? I'll be eighty-seven next month."

We start walking again.

"You're in pretty good shape for a man your age," I says.

"Well, the body's one thing and the soul's another. What I got to worry about is what shape my soul's going to be in when I . . ."

He waves his bony hand like he's waving bye-bye to hisself.

When we go into the rectory, an old woman in a black dress and an apron hurries right up and looks him over like she's making sure the trip from the church ain't wore him out. She's got a light shawl in her hands which she tries to put around his shoulders. There's a brief scuffle as he fights her off.

"For God's sake, Angelina, will you stop fussin' over me?"

"You'll catch a chill."

"I was just outside with nuttin' on. Why would I now get a chill inside the house?"

"You're in a sweat from the walk, so now you'll get a chill in this old drafty house."

"Hoo, hoo, hoo," he says, waving her away and showing me into the library all in the same bunch of motions.

Angelina gives me a look and casts her eyes up to

heaven. What can you do with stubborn old men? she's saying.

It's a great old room, all dark wood and leather, with a Turkey carpet in deep reds on the floor and a huge desk over by these windows what look out into a small garden. It's dark in the room but not what you'd call gloomy. Warm and cozy would be a better word.

"So sit, sit," Father Rocco says. "I'll pour us a couple glasses."

"I don't drink, Father," I says.

"You sick? You' stomach don' feel good?"

"I just never got the taste for it."

"Hokay, so you wan' I have Mrs. Gionelli make you a cup tea, a cup coffee?"

"I'm just fine," I says.

"Hokay," he says again, bringing his glass of wine back with him and sitting down in the leather chair opposite the one I'm sitting in. "So how can I be of service to you, my son?"

"I'm trying to find out what I can about a family what lives in the neighborhood or used to live in the neighborhood."

"What's the name?"

"Tramontina."

He closes his eyes as though what I just said gives him pain or like he's saying a little prayer.

"You know this family?" I says.

"Yes, they are very well known here."

"Why is that?"

"First of all, they are one of the oldest families in the parish. It's an honored name."

"They're good people, then?"

He laughs, his old lips twisting a little bit in a show of disdain.

"You're askin' an old priest to be uncharitable. Like most families—even like most individuals—the Tra-

139

montina family is honored for Christian virtues and respected for evil deeds. There's good and bad in families and in individuals, you understan' wha' I'm sayin'?"

"I understand exactly. I come up against it all the time. You make up your mind somebody's a good person, without a mean bone in their body, and the next thing you know they're doing you or somebody dirt. Another time you're sure somebody's a bad apple and the next thing you know they're taking a beggar into their house to give him something to eat."

Father Rocco's nodding his head. "You never know what they'll do and you never know the reasons they got for doin' what they do. Tha's righ'."

"So, if you had to color them good, color them bad, as a bunch, which would it be?"

"The women are mostly good as women tend to be. Because they become mothers, don' you see? When women do bad, it's usually because of passion or the urgings of the men they're wit'. When men do bad, it's usually because of pride or greed. So with the men is half and half. But when you got some black, which is very strong, it's enough to turn a bucket of white pain' dark gray."

"So who are we talking about here?"

"Salvatore Tramontina's brothers, sons, and nephews."

I wait for him to tell me more because I don't know this Salvatore Tramontina and I know that any story about an old Italian family's going to start back a long time ago.

23

"Is HOKAY I GIVE YOU A LITTLE HISTORY LES-
son abou' Italy and Italians?" Father Rocco says.

"I'd be happy for anything you can tell me."

"It has to do wit' the way people organize themselves
to deal with authority and why these organizations
sometimes grow twisted," he says.

"They grow from a seed of pride and self-protection.
A necessity. They are based on a strong family, a weak
government, and the father as master of the house," he
says.

"Male role model," I says.

"You got it. So where the law is powerless or far away
or won' respond to the people, there's got to be some
place injured parties can go for justice. So a man or a
few men appear among them who has . . . ahhhh . . .
òmerta. You unnerstan'?"

"I know the word but I don't exactly know its meaning," I says.

"A man who has òmerta is more a man than other
men."

"Okay. Charisma."

"Ah, shoo, we got these charismatics in the church. The authorities give them the old one-eye, you unner- stan'? But tha's another subjec'. So, this man decides arguments, distributes favors, levies fines, and hands out punishment. He becomes a middleman, a judge, and sometimes an enforcer, you unnerstan'? To do this he must have the willing cooperation of the people. They must give him their support."

I'm thinking that it sounds a lot like the way a party organization works, only with the kind of organization he's talking about, the power's concentrated at the top and nobody else's got much to say about it.

"He must have their silence. When he can't be assured of their silence, it comes to pass that he finds ways to impose the silence upon them. That's when something that started out a good thing becomes a bad thing," Father Rocco says.

"Sometimes—often—the social organization becomes criminal. It don't happen overnight. It happens in small ways at first, then in larger ways," he says.

"This happened all over the *Mezzogiórno*," he says.

"Uh?" I says.

"The south of Italy," he says.

"You think," he goes on, "that all these criminal orga- nizations are the Mafia. Well, maybe today you're not so wrong. It's like a brand name, you understan' wha' I mean? Like you say Frigidaire which everybody knows is an electric ice box even though there's many other brand names besides Frigidaire. So the Mafia stands for all Italian criminal organizations and fraternities, but there are others. Calabria has the *Onorata Società.*"

"The Honored Society," I says.

"Tha's right. And there is the *Camòrra* which comes from Naples."

Right away I'm thinking of the photographs taken by a photographer in that city.

"Naples is the principal city of Campagnia, and back in 1908, 1910, many people, mostly young men, left their villages in the Campagnia and emigrated to America," he says.

"And the Tramontinas came to Chicago."

"Tha's right. There's five brothers. A couple of them end up living around Grand Avenue which had a lot of Italians in those days. Another settled Back of The Yards and worked in the packing plants. Yet another found work and a home in Holy Name parish."

"The Twenty-fifth Ward," I says.

Here I'm looking at it. Somebody from the Tramontina family, one of the original family, lived in Vito Vellitri's ward and five'll get you ten, somebody from that family still lives there. So, one way or another, Vellitri's got an interest in something to do with his ward, my ward, and probably the Tenth Ward, too.

Father Rocco's got this little smile on his mouth. "You see how it is? We all identify our neighborhood according to what interests us most. You're a politician, so you see the cities broken up into wards, a policeman would see it divided into police areas and districts, and I locate myself according to church parishes."

"That's right, Father," I says. "So the fifth brother settles here in the Tenth."

"In St. Francis de Sales parish. Yes."

"You knew that brother?"

"Salvatore Tramontina. I knew him. I came here from a village not far from Naples as a young priest of twenty-two."

I start to do a quick subtraction in my head, but he does it for me.

"Nineteen twenty-five," he says. "Salvatore Tramontina was a man of twenty-nine or thirty. He had already passed the initiation of dagger, pistol, and wine, which did not, at that time, necessarily mean that he had committed any crimes or would even be asked to do so. It was simply a ceremony of which there are so many among all people at all times."

"I been asked to join a couple of groups what wear funny hats and give each other secret handshakes myself," I says.

"One could say I, too, have been involved with ceremonies tha' use mysterious oaths and ancient symbols."

I like he's got this sense of humor and can laugh about the things he does as part of his faith which some other people could think's a little strange.

"He was a good man," he goes on. "He was already marked to become the *masto* . . . ahhhh . . ."

"Like a Mafia *don?*" I says.

"You understan' Italian?" he asks me.

"A little," I says, measuring a small space with my fingers.

"All right, like a *don* if you keep in mind that Salvatore was a leader in a benevolent society that was genuinely trying to help their people make their way in a strange land with unfamiliar laws."

"But there was police and judges and courts available to everybody. It wasn't like there was a weak government. There was a system that worked."

"More or less," he says, holding up a warning finger.

"Well, as good as most and better than plenty," I says.

"But these immigrants had no language. They were afraid of the police because of the experiences they'd had in their own country. They did not, yet, have so many officers on the force like you Irish."

"So, all right, this *Camòrra* kept the peace in the neighborhoods."

"They did what they could. There were always criminals."

"And did Salvatore Tramontina become a criminal?"

"Never. But there were those among his brothers, sons, nephews, and sons-in-law who did. The next generation and the one after that and then the one after that."

I'm finally getting to something I can grab hold of, something which ain't ancient history but which is now. "You knew Theobald Tramontina?"

He makes a snorting sound through his nose and turns his head away like he's afraid he's going to bust out laughing and spray the last mouthful of wine all over the place. He waves his hand at me again, telling me to cut out being such a funny fellow.

"Teddy. That clown?" he says. "He's always been . . ." He taps the side of his head with his finger.

"Somebody else called him a clown," I says.

"Teddy used to strut around in a black suit, with patent leather shoes and a Borsellino hat, pretending to be *camorrista*," Father Rocco says. "Trying to impress the young women, sitting in the wine shops and saloons pretending to be a dangerous criminal. Nobody took him seriously."

Somebody took him seriously about something, I thought. Somebody killed him. So maybe he wasn't such a clown after all. At least, if he tried to play any heavy games, somebody *thought* he wasn't such a clown.

"I shouldn' make jokes about him," Father Rocco says. "He's not to blame. It was probably the motor car acciden' wha' scrambled the brains in his head."

"He was in an automobile accident?"

"When he was very young. His papa and mama died in a crash coming back from Akron. A tragedy. May they rest in the arms of Jesus," he says, then crosses hisself and presses his thumb to his lips.

"I was told, by the person what told me that he liked

to clown around, that Theobald lives here in the Tenth with his mother."

Father Rocco shakes his head. "They got it wrong. Ever since his mama and papa were killed, he's lived with his aunt, actually his grandfather's unmarried sister."

"How long ago did they move out of your parish?"

Father Rocco looks surprised. "Did they move? I don' know tha'. He never came to church, you understan', and his aunt's very old and don' come to Mass excep' on Christmas and Easter, so I ain' sure, but I don' t'ink they moved. So far as I know they still live over on a Hun'erd and Fit' and Avenue F on the bottom floor of a t'ree flat."

"Well, thank you very much, Father," I says, getting to my feet.

"Tell me," Father Rocco says, "is Theobald in some kind of trouble?"

"Unless I'm very much mistaken, Father, I think that Teddy Tramontina's dead."

24

THE THREE-FLAT OVER ON A HUNDRED AND
fifth and Avenue F is one of the old wooden tenements
with bay windows in the parlor and an enclosed outside
stairway in the back. It's got a neat little front yard, very
nicely kept, with a plaster statue of the Virgin Mary in
her blue robes on the lawn, inside a little shrine made
of gilded wood. It's early in the year for them, but the
days are getting warm and there's blue and white cro-
cuses growing in a border all around the yard.

There's white curtains in the windows of every flat.
You can see that the people what live here got a lot of
pride.

I walk up the steps to the porch and through the door
into the vestibule. The three mail boxes are bright and
polished with neat little tags underneath each one.

Once upon a time you rang the bell under the mailbox
and somebody in the flat would blow into the speaking
tube—which was usually in the kitchen or by the front
door. That made a whistle in the speaking tube by the
boxes telling you it was okay for you to speak, some-

body was listening. Then, if they wanted to let you in, they'd push a button which would release the lock on the inside door and you could get in.

But over the years those bells and buttons and buzzers stopped working in most of these three-flats and two-flats, or the lock on the front door got jimmied or busted and nobody ever bothered to fix them.

So first I try the inside door but it won't give.

I ring the bell for the Tramontina flat. In about a minute the speaker whistles. I put my mouth up close to the mouthpiece in the wall and say, "I would like to speak to Ms. Tramontina."

A voice which says "Eh?" comes faintly out of the mouthpiece which also operates as an earpiece.

I put my mouth closer and yell a little louder. "I would like to have a word with Ms. Tramontina."

There's a muffled rattle of what could be Italian but who could tell the way this system works?

After another minute, while I stand there trying to figure out how I can tell whoever's in the flat what I want, a voice says, "Please state your name and business again."

"My name is Jimmy Flannery and I want to talk with Ms. Tramontina about Theobald Tramontina."

"Who?"

"Her grandnephew. At least that's how the old priest over to St. Francis de Sales described the relationship."

There's a long pause and I'm thinking that maybe that was too many words to be yelling into the dusty old speaking tube all in one string when the buzzer on the door almost catches me off guard. I just manage to grab the handle and shove the door open before the buzzing stops.

I walk a short way down the hall to the front door and stand there waiting for it to open.

I can feel somebody looking me over through the peep hole.

"Who did you say you were?" this woman's voice says from the other side of the door.

"My name's Jimmy Flannery."

"And what do you want? You said you wanted to talk to my uncle? He's not here."

"No, I said I wanted to talk to somebody *about* Theobald Tramontina."

"So, yes, what about him?"

"I think we'd do better if we didn't have to shout through the door."

"I don't know you," she says.

"Well, I can understand how you'd be careful letting strangers into your house. I'm an official with the city, if that means anything."

I reach into my back pocket and take out my wallet which has got my identification in a plastic window and a little badge from the Sewer Department pinned to the leather on the other side. Sometimes you got to get permission to go into houses when sewers are backed up and things like that and you got to have something what proves that you are who you say you are.

I hold it up to the peephole.

"You wait right there," she says.

I wait right there for maybe four minutes, during which time I imagine she's calling somebody she knows who's in the know about city departments—everybody in Chicago knows somebody who's in the know—to check out if a certain Jimmy Flannery works for the city.

The door finally opens up and a very nice-looking woman maybe twenty-five years old steps back and tells me to come in.

She's wearing a cinnamon-colored blouse and a pair

of tapered slacks cut so they break just on top of a pair of high heeled shoes with straps.

The entry hall is very similar to my own, except there's a religious picture on practically every wall and a huge wardrobe with mirrored doors directly opposite the door so it gives you a little start stepping inside and seeing somebody coming toward you before you realize it's yourself.

"Come into the living room and I'll go fetch Nonna," she says.

"If it's all the same to you, could I wait for her in the kitchen?"

She cocks her head and a little smile touches her mouth. She's got a thick head of black hair which is all teased out like a cloud around her head and very red lipstick on her lips.

"Flannery's your name?" she says.

"That's right."

"What else do you do besides inspecting sewers?"

So right there I know she's made the call I thought she'd made, otherwise how would she know I was an inspector and not something else?

"I'm the Democratic Party committeeman in the Twenty-seventh Ward. Why do you ask?"

"I figured you had to be a politician, something like that. Used to meeting the people. It always makes old people feel more comfortable sitting in the kitchen, doesn't it?"

I give her my Jimmy Cagney smile. (Everybody says I look a little bit like him, though I got to tell you I'm several inches taller than he was—God rest his soul.)

"You don't look so old," I says.

"Pop," she says.

"What was that?"

"That was the bird you just charmed falling out of the tree."

150

"Maybe the bird's got a name?"

"Shira. Shira Carmel," she says.

"Your real name?" I asks.

She grins at me. "Which one? Shira or Carmel?" Then she says, "All right, the kitchen it is. Follow me."

"I could probably find it myself," I says. "Blindfolded. This flat's laid out practically the same as mine."

"There's only so many ways to build a railroad," she says.

The kitchen's clean as wax. The old saying "You could eat off the floor" pops right into my head.

There's a very old woman—I'd say she was in her eighties, maybe even ninety—sitting at the kitchen table with her hands in her lap as though she's waiting to be called into the living room. She's wearing a black dress with small purple flowers on it. Her white hair's cut pretty short for a woman her age, parted in the middle and combed back to show off how thick it is. I notice there's no wedding band on her finger.

There's two cups, a little dish of lemon wedges, and a bowl of cube sugar on the table. They was having tea.

"This is Mr. Flannery, Nonna. He wants to speak with us about Uncle Ted."

"Theobald?" the old lady says, and her fingers start to twist around themselves, her eyes looking scared, staring at me like she knows I'm a messenger of bad news.

"Would you like a cup of tea, Mr. Flannery?" Shira asks.

"That would be nice, thank you very much," I says, not really wanting anything, but knowing there's a way to do these things.

"Please to sit down," Nonna says, as Shira goes to the cabinet to get me a cup and then to the stove to pour the tea out of the pot sitting on the burner.

The old lady's got a very heavy accent but at least she speaks American.

"Do you take milk?" Shira asks.

"Just like it is, thank you," I says.

Shira comes around behind me and puts the cup of tea on the table from the side like a waitress would do. Nonna's eyes glance up at Shira over my shoulder and I got a feeling a significant something has passed between them.

"You like *biscotto?*" Nonna asks.

"I love *biscotto,*" I says.

She glances at Shira again, and Shira goes to the cabinet, reaches for a round tin, opens it up, and sets it down on the table nearest me because I'm the guest. Then she sits down.

There's a funny atmosphere in the room like everybody's playing that game we used to play when we was kids where the trick is to make somebody else do the talking so they'll say the secret word what puts them out of the circle.

"So," I says, looking at Shira, "I'm no good at figuring out who's related to who. But—am I right?—you call this lady grandmother?"

"She's actually my great-grandfather's sister, my great-grandaunt. Uncle Teddy's really my granduncle. Why do you want to bother working it out? Do we know you? Do you know us? Do you know Uncle Teddy? Also, my last name's not really Carmel," Shira says in this very harsh manner, "it's Cardello. So now you know everything about us and you still haven't told us why you're here and what you want."

"I'm trying to be careful," I says.

"Careful about what?"

I take out the picture from the health club.

"Is this your Uncle Teddy?" I asks.

Shira looks at it and becomes very agitated. She

pushes it across the oilcloth on the table so it's in front of the old lady who gives a little gasp, her eyes welling up as she starts to tremble. She's in awful distress. She says something very fast in Italian.

Shira jumps up and leaves the room.

She's back in a minute with a bottle in her hand. She opens it up and squeezes three drops of medicine into the old lady's tea. Then she has to help her raise the cup to Nonna's mouth, the old lady's shaking so bad. What color she's got comes back into Nonna's cheeks.

Shira runs her hand across the old lady's forehead then turns to me and says, "Where is he?"

"You mind telling me how long he's been missing?"

"A month. Maybe a month."

"And you never filed a missing person?"

"I would've done, but Nonna and some other members of the family wouldn't have it."

"Why not?"

"Because old country people like to take care of their own by themselves," she practically shouts at me, she's so upset about me asking all these questions and not answering the one important question she asked me.

"Will you please answer my goddam question? Where's my uncle?"

I get on my feet, because the way the old lady looks, I'm scared that something terrible will happen when I tell them. I'm sorry I ever stuck my nose in. If there's one thing I don't envy cops, it's having to go tell people that somebody in their family's been hurt or killed.

"Please," I says, "would you just tell me what kind of medicine you just gave her?"

"It's for her heart. You can imagine at her age. Her heart. Other things . . ."

She stops talking, standing there like she's helpless in the face of what she already knows I'm going to tell her.

"I'm afraid I got some very bad news for you," I says.

"I'm probably not the one should be telling you, but I don't see how I can do anything else."

Nonna's face goes whiter than it already is and she sways a little in the chair.

"I'm afraid Teddy's dead," I says.

Shira makes a sound like I'd punched her in the stomach, but now that the bad news is out, the old lady sort of pulls herself together and all the shaking stops. It's like she reached down inside herself and pulled out this cloak of strength and calm which she wraps around herself. She lets out a long sigh like she's turning off the tears, too.

"You all right, Ms. Tramontina?" I says.

"Nonna," Shira says, getting down on her knees so she can embrace the old woman.

"Ah, ah, ah," Nonna says, patting Shira on the back, like she was a child in need of comfort.

"I'm sorry I had to give you that shock but—"

"Then why did you?" Shira asks me, whirling around, her dark eyes glaring at me, angry enough to bite off my head.

"You're right. I shouldn't've come here asking about Theobald. But he died right in front of my eyes. There wasn't any identification on him. There wasn't any missing persons report that fit his description. Nobody seemed to know who he was. I guess I'm just the kind of person hates to see somebody lost out there like that with nobody to care. But you're right, I shouldn't've come here on my own."

Shira gets up and stands there trembling a little, her body getting rid of the adrenaline rush, her face smoothing out and her eyes cooling down.

"But I came," I goes on, "and when I get what I was looking for—when I find Theobald's family—I just don't see how I could get up and say thank you very much and leave you sitting here wondering what it was all about."

Shira sits down and looks at me like she ain't finished telling me what she thinks of what I done, but Nonna says, "Hush, hush, hush," and reaches out to soothe her again.

"My rosary," the old lady says. "Will you get my rosary?"

Shira acts like she's glad of the chance to leave the room.

"What can you tell me about Theobald?" I asks, because I know it does people good to talk at times like this.

Nonna's face gets this wistful expression on it, like she's remembering what it was like when her Theobald was small.

"He was a good boy. He was foolish but he was a good boy. He lost his mama and papa."

"Father Rocco told me."

"I nursed him. I raised him. He was not *like* my own son. He *was* my own son. He had a sunny nature. He did no harm."

"I'm not thinking so much about when he was a kid. I'm thinking about when he grew up."

A smile gives a wry little twist to her dry old lips. "Nobody ever took him serious. His uncles and his cousins gave him work now and then, but they never took him serious."

"What kind of work?"

"They're in olive oil import-export, the wholesale grocery business, the commercial laundry business. A lot of different businesses."

I'll just bet, I'm thinking. She's naming the businesses that gangster types usually muscle in on and take over. Lots of chances to apply pressure when you need more customers. Lots of transportation around to use for hijacking when you want a little something extra. Plenty of access to docks and warehouses.

I'm wondering if this old woman, who's lived so long, expects me to believe she don't know what illegal activities her relatives could be involved in. She's looking at me with a very shrewd expression in her eye and then she does me the honor of showing me she don't take me for a fool.

"Nothing like that," she said. "They wouldn't trust him, with anything like that. They thought he was a fool. A clown. That he was . . . *deteriorare.*"

"Impaired. Retarded," Shira says, coming back into the kitchen.

"Was he?" I says.

She goes to the table and hands Nonna a set of blue prayer beads which the old lady immediately begins to work through her fingers. Shira'd been gone longer than it would've taken to pick up a set of beads so I figured she'd been on the telephone again.

She's looking at me, trying to read my mind.

"He was different," she says. "Smart about some things, not so smart about others."

"Ain't we all?" I says.

"He was an actor," Nonna says, smiling ruefully.

"A harmless clown," Shira says.

Somebody maybe didn't think he was so harmless, I think to myself again. Unless it turns out he really did die of just a heart attack. But if that's all it was, Hackman would've said so straight out without any hints left over.

Shira stands up.

"I think, maybe, you better go now, Mr. Flannery."

She walks me down the hall to the front door and opens it for me. I stop a minute in the doorway.

"I'd just like to know if Mr. Tramontina could've got in the way of somebody who wouldn't hesitate to—"

"What?" Shira asks, starting to get angry again.

"—do him an injury."

"Rub him out?" Shira says, in this sarcastic tone of voice. "Isn't that what the wops and guineas do, rub each other out? Isn't that what you people think, that all Italians are associated with criminals . . . ?"

I get a feeling that her outrage is more than a little put on. Maybe she's just trying to drive me out the door and maybe Theobald wasn't the only actor in the family.

". . . if not actually members of the Mafia."

"Or the *Camòrra*," I says, and then I'm out the door.

I hurry down the block to a little grocery store. They got a public phone on the wall. I take out the card Vellitri give me and dial his private number. There's a busy signal.

I don't think that Vito Vellitri gets very many calls on his private number on a Sunday afternoon.

I don't think, anymore, that Shira was calling my office when she kept me waiting at the door.

25

MONDAY I GET A CALL FROM MARY AT WORK. She tells me she won't be home for supper so I should either warm up what's left of Sunday dinner—which is in the fridge—or I should catch a bite out in some salad bar.

Instead I catch a hamburger and some fries at a greasy spoon on the way over to the storefront where I'm holding my weekly open house for precinct captains and anybody what needs my help.

When I open the door, I'm hit by all this female giggling and laughter. I see some of my precinct captains, but mostly the waiting room's filled with women and pregnant girls.

McGuire's sitting in a chair against the wall between the door to Janet Canarias's office and the assistant's office—which I've been using—with his arms folded like he don't know what to do.

When he sees me, his face lights up and he hurries on over.

"I don't know what to tell you, Jimmy."

"All these pregnant girls here to talk to me?" I asks.

"Well, I don't know about that, but I guess you're going to get the credit for helping them, no matter they talk to you, they don't talk to you."

"Just exactly what is going on?" I asks.

"Your wife's in the alderman's—alderwoman's—office examining these young women. She tells me she's talked it over with Ms. Canarias and it's all right with her. So now, she says, all she's got to do is find out if it's all right with you."

"I'll tell you, McGuire," I says, "she'll talk to me, but I got an idea I ain't got a thing to say about it."

Just then the door to the big office opens up and Millie Jefferson hustles a girl out the door, then reaches out her hand and points a finger at the next patient.

"Hold on there just a second, will you, Millie?" I says, walking on over. "Would you mind asking my wife if she can spare me a minute?"

Hearing my voice, Mary calls out from inside, "Come on in, James. I've always got a minute for you."

I hurry into the office and shut the door.

Mary's sitting in Janet's swivel chair, which she's pulled out from behind the desk, and she's got on a white coat and a stethoscope around her neck.

"What's going on here, Mary?"

"I found a place where these girls won't have to walk up and down six flights of stairs."

"So, instead, *you* end up walking up and down six flights of stairs."

She gives me a smile, trying to butter me up a little bit.

"My husband'll carry me when I can't make it anymore."

"I'd carry you if I could, and it's very sweet of you to think I got the strength, but the truth is, Mary, I can hardly make it up them six flights of stairs myself nowadays."

"We can always get a neighbor to help you. You can make a fireman's seat out of your arms. You know what I mean. Where you grab the other person's wrists and—"

"I know how it works, Mary. I'm just saying I don't know what you got in mind here. The closer it gets to the time when you should be getting plenty of rest, you're taking on more and more work and responsibility."

"I can't just turn my back," she says.

"I understand, but you can't save the world either."

"I'm not trying to save the world, James. I'm just trying to help the few I can. Just like you try to do."

"All right, I can't give you an argument on that, but you start helping out with these women now, where's it going to end?"

"What do you mean?"

"I mean what comes after? So you do what you can to teach them to take care of themselves before the babies're born. Maybe you arrange for them to get a better diet. You get them some vitamin shots. You get a midwife in to stand by while they have the babies. Maybe you even get some of them into the maternity ward of some hospital. But what happens after? Where's all the money coming from to see the babies get the right nutrition, they don't end up eating paint loaded with lead when they start to teethe while they're being raised in flats full of cockroaches and rats?"

"Like you say, James, we can't save the world. All we can do is what we can do, but we have to try and do it. Don't get mad at me."

"Oh, I ain't mad at you, Mary," I says. "Sometimes I just get mad at the way the system works. I feel like a kid with a spoon trying to bail out Lake Michigan. And the worst of it is, the spoon's got a lot of holes in it."

"So, then, it's all right with you if I go on seeing these

women on Monday night while you've got the use of the office?"

"What can I say?" I says, because what can I say?

I go out into the main office to start seeing the people who're there to see me, and who's standing there with this cat-what-ate-the-canary grin on his kisser but Billy Behan.

"So, I wondered how long it was going to take before you and your wife joined forces to subvert the legitimate concerns of the welfare system and use the resources of a prenatal care clinic for the dissemination of information on birth control, the dispensation of condoms to minors from a federal and state funded facility, and the distribution of instruction on how and where to seek abortion."

"I don't know exactly what you're talking about, Billy," I says. "All I do know is that you're sounding just like a lawyer and I don't speak that language. You just come on into my office and let me buy you a cup of coffee and a doughnut. We can put our feet up and talk this over."

"I don't have to put my feet up, Flannery. My feet don't hurt."

"Well, if you don't start acting like a human being and stop acting like a horse's ass, they're going to hurt when I step on your shoe shine. I'm willing to put up with a lot to let everybody have their say, but you're pushing my patience to the edge and I want to sit down and talk over our differences."

I go into the office and he follows me. I pour him a cup of coffee. "You take sugar? You take creamer? You take artificial sweetener?"

"Black," he says.

"Spoken like a real newshound," I says. "How about a doughnut? We got sugared. We got cinnamon. We got glazed and we got sticky."

"Uh?" he says, but I got the box of doughnuts shoved under his nose, so he looks them over and grabs a sticky.

I take a jelly and a cup of coffee with artificial sweetener and nondairy creamer in it and sit down behind the desk.

"I seem to remember an article you got printed, coming out against abortion," I says. "You figure women got no right to make that choice?"

"I didn't come out against free choice. I came out against the taxpayer footing the bill for abortions on demand."

"Okay, I understand. So what you're against ain't a woman who can afford it having an abortion, only poor women who can't afford it."

"I'm against encouraging promiscuity among the underprivileged and uneducated."

"So, let me see if I get your meaning. You're saying these young women—these poor, uneducated women— go out there and get pregnant because they can go get it taken care of?"

"Abortion on demand."

"So, you think to them it's like getting their teeth cleaned. They don't think anything about getting rid of a baby. They don't wrestle with their consciences. They just make babies for the fun of it and then go get their teeth cleaned, in a manner of speaking."

"I don't think the taxpayers should pay for it and I don't think the community should encourage such behavior."

"Well, the community encourages the behavior with moving pictures, music lyrics, rock concerts, and advertising—things that make a buck—but they don't do much to mitigate the consequences like funding programs to take care of these babies you want these poor children to have. You don't even want high schools to

hand out condoms or for them to be advertised on radio
and television."

"What?"

"You see, I can talk like a lawyer when I got to just
like you can. But talking like a lawyer and ignoring
common sense don't make things right," I says.

"What makes things right is morality, faith in God,
and following the instruction of the church," Behan
says.

"The Catholic church, is that right, Billy?" I says.

"That's right," he says.

"Everybody should follow the teachings of the Roman
Catholic Church?" I says.

"It wouldn't do anybody any harm," he says.

"Even most Catholics don't follow all the teaching of
the Catholic church, Billy, and you know it," I says.
"But I ain't going to argue the moral issues here because
that means we got to first agree on what morality really
is. Who lays down the rules. Things like that. So, what
I'm going to say is just this: there's a lot of poor, uneducated girls and women out there worried sick about
what's right for them to do and, keep the babies or don't
keep the babies, they need help to do whatever they
decide, with the least pain and sickness possible. That's
what Mary's trying to do and that's what I'm trying to
do."

He's finished the doughnut and now he's sucking on
his fingertips one after the other, trying to lick the sugar
off.

"You want a napkin?" I asks.

He reaches into his pocket and takes out a handkerchief. He wipes his hands. "That's okay," he says.

"What I'm saying is that we're going to tell our
friends and neighbors how to terminate their pregnan-
cies the safest way—if that's what they decide to do—
and we're going to give them all information we can

give them about how to take care of themselves before they have the babies—if that's what they want—and how to take care of the babies, keep them fed and clean and warm, even though they ain't got any money, every chance we get."

"So, okay," Behan says, standing up. "You told me and now I'm telling you. I ain't going to discuss the moral issues either. I'm a good Catholic and you're a fall-away Catholic. So, talking to you from that angle would be like talking to a stone. So all I'm going to say is this: I'm interested in the misuse of public grants and funds. Malfeasance in office, elected or appointed. And other matters concerning the commonweal—"

"The public good," I says, letting him know I ain't dazzled with his command of the language.

"—according to the laws of the city, state and country. So if I find out you or your wife's spending public funds earmarked for prenatal instruction on materials teaching contraception, I'll blow the whistle on you."

"Do what you got to do, Billy," I says, getting to my feet, too. "But while you're doing it, I'm just asking you—"

"Warning me?"

"—*asking* you to have a care about the way you go about it. I don't want you scaring any of these ladies with your questions and innuendos. Don't be like those reporters on TV what shove a microphone into the faces of people what are in terrible trouble, full of worry and pain, and ask them how they're feeling."

And that's all we got to say to each other right then. He leaves and I'm so upset I have another jelly doughnut.

26

WHEN I GO OUT TO SEE WHO'S WAITING TO see me, McGuire's sitting there grinning like the cat what ate the canary. Two little people are sitting with him, like he's a big book between a couple of small bookends. He holds up a finger to them, telling them to please stay put and swaggers over to me.

"I got what you been asking for," he says.

"What's that?"

"A line on that gamoosh what went missing. These people live downstairs from such a person as you described to me and I described to people in my precinct."

"They live in the Twenty-seventh?"

"That's correct. Right over on Justine and Arbor Place."

"Well, you certainly done good, ain't you, Dan? Ask them do they want a cup of coffee or tea and bring them on in."

I go into the office and pretty soon there's a knock on the door. I say, "Come in," and McGuire ushers in the two people who are holding a couple of cups of coffee in their hands.

I stand up and give them a big smile.

"Mr. and Mrs. Amico," McGuire says, "this here's Mr. James Flannery, the Democratic Party committeeman of the Twenty-seventh Ward. He's the man to see if you want something done."

"You mean to tell us," Mr. Amico says, "I been wasting my time talking to my landlord about the heat and the noise upstairs? This is the man I should've been talking to all the time?"

"Well, not exactly, Mr. Amico," I says, shaking his hand. "What Mr. McGuire means is, when you got no other place to turn, you can always come to me. If it's something to do with city government and services, I probably can do something for you. If it's a private situation, I might be able to talk to somebody for you or give you some advice, or even if I can't do nothing for you, I can give you a sympathetic ear."

"So, that's something?" Mrs. Amico says, but I don't know if that's a statement of approval or a kind of sarcastic observation.

I shake her hand, too, and says, "What I'm trying to say here, Mrs. Amico, is that I try to be a good neighbor."

"We could use a good neighbor," she says. "Across the hall we got a couple with three kids, ride their trikes in the hallways, run around like wild Indians."

"Downstairs we got a young couple—"

"Could just be living together, not even married," Mrs. Amico interrupts her husband.

McGuire has arranged chairs and everybody finally sits down, the Amicos still complaining about everybody in the apartment building until Mr. Amico says, "The ones upstairs was the worst."

"How many people do you think was living in the apartment upstairs?" I asks.

"Who knows?" he says. "Sometimes it sounded like half a dozen one right after the other. All hours of the night. Flushing the toilet six, seven times in a row."

"You ever see people going in and out?"

"This was at night. This was at one, two o'clock in the morning. Decent people are in bed," Mr. Amico said.

"What do you think, my husband and me should've crouched out on the landing in our nightclothes, spying on our neighbors?" Mrs. Amico says.

"I don't think that would've been a good idea," I says, "and I ain't suggesting. I just wondered who you saw."

"Just the one man, the one Mr. McGuire here described to us."

"You know his name?"

"Never heard, he never told us, and there wasn't any name on his door or the mailbox."

"You seen or heard him lately?"

"No. That's just it. That's just what we was talking about in the grocery store—when this man, McGuire here, starts asking us questions—"

"And shoving pictures of naked men under my nose."

"The man was in a pair of athletic shorts, Mrs. Amico," I says.

"All the same it ain't right, handing around pictures of a person in his underwear," Mr. Amico says. "Anyways we was telling the grocer how this neighbor—who lives up over our heads and was so noisy practically every night—all of a sudden stops making any noise at all."

"We was worried," she says.

"You call the police?"

They both look startled as though I'd suggested something weird to them.

167

"What would we be doing calling the police? What king of neighbors you think we are? We mind our own business," he says with some indignation.

" 'Live and let live' is our motto," she says.

"You talk to the super?"

"The what?"

"The superintendent of the building."

"What superintendent? A manager comes around once a month to collect the rents. The owner is God-only-knows where."

"How long has it been since you saw or heard the man Mr. McGuire described?"

"The last he was home was a week ago Saturday."

"He never came home Saturday night. So the last time we heard him—we didn't see him—was on the Friday," she says.

"You ever have a talk with him?"

"Once," Mr. Amico says.

"When was that."

"Maybe a week after he moved in."

"You bump into him on the stairway, in the hallway, in the elevator?"

"I went up and knocked on his door. He was already making noise at night."

"Walking around without his slippers. Flushing the toilet," she chips in.

"So you knocked on his door. What time was this?"

"Who remembers?" he says.

"It was around ten o'clock in the morning," she says.

"Okay," he says, "that sounds about right. I knocked on the door around ten and he yells, 'Just a minute,' and I know he's looking me over through the peephole. Then he asks me through the door what do I want and I says I'm his neighbor downstairs and I'm there to bid him welcome and talk to him about the thin floors and noisy toilets we got to suffer with in the building . . ."

"And?" I says, because he's stopped talking and needs a nudge. I can tell he's remembering the occasion and he's getting angry all over again like he must've done when it happened.

"And this bozo looks me up and down, giving me this oily smile, and tells me I got any complaints I should go talk to the owner. Then he shuts the door in my face."

"A person like that, didn't even have a decent living-room suit," she says.

"Living-room suit?" I says.

"You know, a couch, a couple chairs, a coffee table. The usual," she says.

"There was a folding card table and bridge chair in the living room. No rugs on the floor," he says.

"No wonder he made so much noise when he walked around without his slippers, all hours of the night," she added.

"You happen to know the name of the manager or the owner of the building?" I asks.

They look at each other, checking to see if the other one knows what he or she don't know. Then she goes into her purse and comes out with a ragged little notebook.

"Would you mind writing it down for me?" I asks, pushing over a pen and a piece of paper.

She finds the page and copies down the names, addresses, and telephone numbers in the same childish writing I saw on the note of complaint in Mr. Tramontina's possession.

When she's finished, I look it over.

The manager is the Arnold Management Company which has got offices at an address over on Randolph. The owner is a Mr. Charles Bucker, lives in Sauganash. He also has a telephone number.

"I want to thank you very much for coming in and

talking to me this way," I says. "If you want to finish your coffee outside or have another cup, help yourself. I'd like to talk to Mr. McGuire for a minute and then he'll drive you home."

I stand up and they stand up and we shake hands all around again and then Mr. Amico says, "Hey."

"Yes?" I says.

"You happen to have a sweet roll to go with the coffee?"

"There's doughnuts in that box right over there," I says.

After they toddle out the door with a doughnut in each hand, I sit there thinking about what they told me.

McGuire looks thoughtful, too.

"Sounds to me like somebody up there was having a poker game or maybe a crap game," McGuire says.

"It'd be nice if that's all it turned out to be," I says, "but I think it could be something a lot more serious. We'll see. I want you to go out there and see that the Amicos got what they want and then run them home. Will you do that? I'm going to make a couple of calls. When you come back I might be gone, maybe for an hour, maybe more, and I'd like you to hold down the fort."

McGuire acts very pleased that I'm asking him to sit in my chair for an hour.

When he leaves, I dial the first number, which is the all-night emergency number of the property management company.

27

THE EMERGENCY NUMBER IS A MESSAGE ON A
machine what tells me that if there's a fire or a gas leak
or any other potential natural disaster, I should call 911.
If it's a complaint or a request, I should wait until after
ten o'clock in the morning every day except Sunday. If
it's something else that just can't wait, I should call . . .
and it gives me another telephone number to call.

This gets me another message on another machine—
or the same machine if they got both lines coming into
it and two outgoing message reels—what asks me if I'm
absolutely sure what I'm calling about can't wait until
morning or until Monday, whichever. It goes on to say
if such is the case, I should call another number if I'm
calling in the evening after five-thirty during the week
or after noon on Saturday or any time Sunday.

On the next go-round I finally get a human voice, a
woman. She don't identify the number of the Arnold
Management Company, she just says, "Hello."

"Am I speaking to the Arnold Management Company?"

"I was hoping you wouldn't ask that," she says.

"I beg your pardon," I says.

"It's six-fifteen," she says. "My husband and I were just going out to dinner and this week we had to take an extra turn covering the company emergency number because Harry Fisk had to go to Cleveland to see a sick relative."

"I'm sorry about that."

"It happened at the last minute, otherwise we never wouldn've made plans to go out to dinner."

"I can understand that."

"I told Jack not five minutes ago that we'd better get a move on or the phone would surely ring."

"That sort of thing happen a lot?"

"Well, enough that I was expecting it."

"I wonder if I could talk to your husband?"

"Why would you want to do that?"

"Well, to ask him if he could help me out with this little problem I've got."

"If you've got a problem with any of the properties which Arnold Management manages, I'm the one to talk to."

"Oh, I'm sorry, I just assumed your husband worked for Arnold's."

"Haven't you heard about women's equality?" she says, not angry, not even annoyed, but just pulling my leg a little.

"I don't know how to apologize for making the mistake."

"You can apologize by telling me the truth. Are you sure whatever you want to complain about can't wait until tomorrow morning?"

"It's not actually a complaint."

"An emergency?"

"Not exactly."

"So what is it then?"

"I think one of your tenants has gone missing from

his apartment in the building you manage on Justine and Arbor Place," I says.

"What make you say that?"

"I was talking to a couple of his neighbors and they told me there wasn't any noise coming from his apartment."

"How would they know?"

"He lives right over their heads."

"That would be the Amicos, right?"

"That's right."

"They send us letters."

"Well, the man upstairs ain't making any noise."

"You think he dropped dead in there?"

"Well, I'm almost certain he dropped dead, but not in the apartment."

"So, where?"

"In a health club."

"So, why are you calling us?"

"I'd like to have a look inside the apartment."

"Oops," she says.

"Oops?"

"You official? Are you a cop or something?"

"I guess you could say I'm a something. I'm a superintendent in Streets and Sanitation, Department of Sewers."

"Are you telling me there's a toilet backed up?"

"We don't know. It wouldn't hurt to have a look."

"So, how long can it take to run into a bathroom and see if the toilet's backed up?"

"Not hardly a minute."

"Will you have identification on you?" she asks.

"I always carry identification. A photo-bearing ID and a city badge."

"That's good. I've seen enough city credentials to know if they're genuine."

"How will I recognize you?" I asks.

"I'm blond and my husband's big," she says.

"Can I have a name, just so I shouldn't walk up and greet the wrong people by mistake."

"I don't know if many blond women and big men'll be hanging around Justine and Arbor. But okay, it's Mabel and Jack. Mabel and Jack Bukowski."

"So you'll meet me at the apartment building?"

"All right, but let's be quick about it."

"I know, your husband made reservations."

Her voice gets confidential. "Well, he didn't really make reservations," she says. "I just told you that in case you were one of those people who were in a hurry just because they wanted to be in a hurry."

"So, I'll meet you at the building," I says. "Say in fifteen minutes?"

I hang up and go out to the reception area. McGuire ain't back yet, but Millie Jefferson's there ready to call in another pregnant girl. I hold up my hand like I'm a traffic cop and ask her will she take over my office, too, and field any requests until Dan McGuire comes back.

"How come you nominated McGuire to stand in for you if you have to go somewhere?" she asks.

"Because you seemed to be busy with other things," I says. "I didn't know I was going somewhere, anyway. Besides, if you start scolding me about ignoring you because you're black, because you're a female, or because you wear a size six dress, I ain't going to listen to it."

She gives me a smile and a slap on the sleeve and asks me what do I know about ladies' dress sizes.

28

I'M WAITING IN FRONT OF THE APARTMENT building about five minutes when a big maroon Cadillac about four years old pulls up to the curb.

Mabel's blond and Jack's big, just like she said.

I stick my hand out as they walk up to me.

"Okay," Mabel says, "let me see."

I take out my wallet and she looks at the badge and inspects the ID.

"Jimmy Flannery," she says. "Haven't I heard of you?"

"Are you a Democrat?"

"That's how we're registered," her husband says, as though I asked a question that was really none of my business.

"The only reason I ask is because if you was Democrats, I figured you might have heard of me. I was just recently elected the committeeman of this ward."

Bukowski suddenly smiles. "Sure, we heard of you. You're the guy who found that gorilla a place to sleep in a bathhouse and she killed two people."

"Well, no, it turned out she didn't kill nobody. The people what killed those two men tried to make it *look* like Baby done it."

"That's right. Also you're the man who found out how old Father Mulrooney from St. Pat's was murdered."

"He wasn't murdered. It was an accident."

"Was it?" he says, frowning, trying to figure out how he got his facts wrong twice in a row.

"So, you remember Father Mulrooney?" I says, trying to get things back on track.

"Well, certainly, we live in the parish," Mabel says. "We sent our sons to St. Ulric's Seminary for Boys."

"So you live in the Fourteenth?"

"That's right," Bukowski says.

"I'm sorry I had to pull you so far out of the way at supper time."

"That's all right. You can make good time on the Dan Ryan after the rush. Say, don't I recall you were involved in the arrest of that photographer who killed that model, or have I got that wrong, too?"

"No, you got that right."

Mabel sort of turns herself sideways and murmurs over her shoulder like we're all three part of a conspiracy and got to keep our voices down. "You can tell us, Mr. Flannery. Is this business about you being a sewer inspector just a cover?"

"A cover?" I says, pretending I don't quite understand what she's saying, but letting it show that I'm only acting.

"You know. We read a lot about undercover cops and . . . well, you know."

"I'd rather not say," I says, glancing over my shoulder like I expect some criminal to be lurking in the shadows.

"So you want to go up and look at the *toilet?*" she says. I'm surprised she don't give me a wink.

"That'd be a good idea," I says.

The door to the vestibule is open but there's a security lock on the inner door. Mabel opens up with a key on a ring of twenty or thirty keys. We go up to the fifth in the elevator.

It's not a fancy building inside, but at least the mailboxes are intact, the glass unbroken, and the floors clean. The only graffitti on the wall is the notice that "Billy's got the hots for Millie" written in red chalk on the wall next to the elevator door.

The elevator chugs up to the fifth floor and we go to the door of 5A.

Mabel knocks. After a minute she knocks a little harder. Then she takes a ledger from her purse and riffles through the pages until she finds the one she wants. This time when she knocks she also calls out, "Mr. Neromano."

Another minute goes by.

"I think you gave him sufficient notice," I says. "You're within your rights to use your passkey."

She picks another key from the ring and fits it into the keyhole, then pushes the door open.

The roller shades have been pulled down almost all the way so it's very gloomy inside, almost dark. I feel for the light switch on the wall by the door and flick it on.

An overhead fixture with three twenty-watt bulbs goes on, showing us a nearly empty room, just like the Amicos'd told me.

There's one of them folding cardboard and vinyl card tables set up underneath the fixture with some writing paper, a couple of ball point pens, and ink pad, and a raw potato on it. There's two folding chairs at the table and another over by the window with a newspaper laying on the floor next to it.

"Are you going to check the toilet?" Mabel asks, and when I look at her, she finally gives me the wink. Well, I figure it's better to let her think what she wants to think and save me asking any more favors.

I go through the short hall from the living room. The bathroom's on one side of it.

I lift the lid. There's the wrapper from a double-edged razor blade floating in it.

"So, that's all right," Mabel says.

They watch me while I check the medicine cabinet—which has a can of shaving cream, a safety razor, a pack of Gillette's, a jar of salve for hemorrhoids, a tooth-brush, and a tube of toothpaste in it—like they want to be sure not to miss a trick. They're going to have a story to tell about watching an undercover detective at work.

The only other thing in the bathroom is a couple of towels and a washcloth.

They trail me like a couple of ducks out to the kitchen. No table, no chairs, just a twenty-gallon trash can with a plastic garbage bag in it filled with the cartons from take-out food; some pizza boxes and some fried chicken cartons, but mostly them little white cartons with the wire handles from Chinese restaurants.

The Bukowskis must think I'm some kind of idiot poking through the garbage the way I'm doing, or maybe they seen enough television to know how a good cop goes about a search.

Smashed into a mess of pizza crusts and chicken bones I find a medicine bottle. It looks just like the medicine bottle Shira brought from the bedroom when Nonna had her spell. I wipe it off with my handkerchief and put it in my pocket. I ain't worried about messing up any fingerprints. The way it was covered with grease and tomato paste there ain't going to be any.

I go on looking.

There's a tall box of paper cups on the drainboard, a plastic squeeze bottle of dishwashing liquid, a plate, two coffee mugs, and two place settings of cheap stainless cutlery. Also a half-full jar of powdered creamer and a carton of artificial sweetener.

In the refrigerator there's a jar of instant coffee, a six-

pack of beer with three cans missing, and a bottle of
low-fat milk what's gone bad.

In the freezer compartment there's a couple of dinners
which've been in there long enough to gather a quarter
inch of frost.

It's pretty clear Tramontina wasn't intending to stay
forever.

Next I trot down the hall and into the bedroom.

There's a single mattress on the floor made up with
sheets and blankets.

A couple of pairs of socks and sets of underwear, a
work shirt and a pair of wash slacks are piled in a cardboard carton in the corner.

Another cardboard box in another corner has a half
dozen shirts, different colors, several sets of underwear
and several pairs of socks, plus a few clean handker-
chiefs in it.

"Aren't you going to check the closet?" Mabel says,
when it looks like I'm going to pass it by.

"Oops," I says. "I ain't used to having civilians watch
me work."

Instead of taking the hint, the Bukowskis smile at
each other like they're really pleased to be getting a look
behind the scenes of a genuine police investigation.

I open the door to the closet. There's a pair of black
dress shoes on the top shelf. There's a very nice sweater,
a topcoat, a raincoat, two sports jackets, two pairs of
slacks, and two suits on hangers. For my taste everything's a little too sharp, too gaudy, the chalk stripes a
little too wide, the colors a little too bright, but it con-
firms the description people gave me about how Theobald Tramontina dressed. There's even a Borsellino hat
on the hook behind the door.

I quickly go through the jacket pockets. Nothing.

So I go back to the living room. I'm out of ideas. I
wander over to the card table and take a look at what

Tramontina was writing. Even from a distance the hand-writing's very familiar. I take the piece of paper on which Mrs. Amico wrote the names and addresses and there it is. Tramontina was trying to copy Mrs. Amico's handwriting.

I'm wondering what we got here, a retarded—or at least a mentally impaired man—practicing to be a forger?

I read about these people they used to call idiot savants—which they got a nicer name for now—what can play the piano like a professional or add up columns of numbers in their heads or paint great pictures but they can't even tie their shoelace. So maybe Tramontina had a special talent like that.

I read the words on the sheet of paper he was working on.

It says: "Respectfully, I take pen in hand to advise you to give the deepest consideration to what I propose. You would be so kind as to gather ten thousand dollars in small unmarked bills . . ." And that's where it ends.

I pick up the potato. Somebody's carved it so it could be used as a rubber stamp. I can remember Mrs. Hindeman, the art teacher, teaching us how to do that in the third grade. The thing that Tramontina carved was a little hand.

Then it hits me what the name he gives the management company when he signed the lease means in English. Neromano. Black hand.

I don't think it'll do any harm to the evidence, so I ink the potato on the ink pad and make an impression on a piece of paper, which I fold up and put into my pocket, the eyes of the Bukowskis on me every minute.

"Well, I guess that's all we can do right now. You better be ready for a call from the police," I says.

"You said you were the police."

"No, I never said that. What I'm talking about here is the *regular* police."

"Oh," she says, and gives me another wink like she knows I'm working undercover.

29

DOWNSTAIRS, I SHAKE HANDS WITH BOTH OF them and ask them to keep whatever they seen quiet for a while, which they say they'll be glad to do.

"I'm sorry I made you late for your supper," I says.

"It was worth it," Mabel says.

"It sure was," her husband says. "Anything else you want, just give us the word."

"I'll do that," I says, and watch them as they get into their car and drive off.

I'm standing there deciding what I should do next and I've about made up my mind that I'd better get right over to the twelfth and let Captain Pescaro in on what I found out, when I see these two familiar figures walking kitty-corner across the street.

Ginger and Finks stop on either side of me.

"You want to have an espresso with Mr. Vellitri?" Ginger asks.

"Just what I had in mind," I says. "I'll follow you in my car."

"No, no, we'll drive you back. Your car'll be all right

parked on the street. You got it locked up, ain't you? You can't ever be too careful nowadays."

We walk across the street and get into the black sedan they drive around in when they're running Vellitri's errands.

I enjoy the ride over to Vellitri's office in the Twenty-fifth. The sedan purrs like a kitten. Nothing like my old clunker.

"What kind of car is this?" I asks.

"Lincoln Town Car."

"It's got a very smooth ride."

"Forty K without specials," Finks says, "and this baby's got specials. You thinking of buying one now that you're a ward leader?"

"Who could afford?"

Ginger pulls up at the curb and Finks hops out so he can open the door for me. I usually don't get such service from these two, so I know that Vellitri's warned them that they better treat me with respect. I'm beginning to feel better and better about being up here closer to the top.

Vellitri's in his office, which looks like it belongs to a cardinal or a senator or a big-time criminal lawyer at least. He stands up to offer me his hand when I walk in.

"Have a chair, Jimmy. Can I offer you a cappuccino, and espresso, a caffe con latte?"

"I could use a glass of water."

"Sparkling or plain?"

"Whichever."

"Evian, Crystal Springs, or Perrier?"

"Whatever."

"Ginger, bring Mr. Flannery a Perrier. Ice?"

"That'd be good," I says.

"And the same for me," he says, as though we're going to have a party and he wants to get into the spirit of things. He sits down.

"Where's your little dog?"

"Alfie? He's at home with my wife. Ever since she started staying home—"

"You're going to have a baby soon," he says.

"That's right. Ever since then, Alfie would just as soon not bum around with me. I take him for his walks but he likes to hang out with Mary."

"That's nice," Vellitri says, as though he's giving me and Mary and my dog a blessing.

Ginger's back with our refreshments.

The water on ice comes in heavy crystal highball glasses on a tray, with what's left in the bottles and a silver bucket of ice cubes with little silver tongs in case we want to add more.

Vellitri nods and waves Ginger and Finks out of the room.

"Are you surprised that my boys were waiting for you outside the apartment house?"

"Well, I got to admit, Mr. Vellitri, I—"

"Vito, please, Jimmy. It's appropriate we should call each other by our Christian names."

"I was giving you the respect due you."

"Due my white hairs. I understand. But you're not a boy anymore. I appreciate your good manners, but I think it should be Vito and Jimmy from now on. Is that agreeable?"

"Yes, sir."

"Vito."

"Vito."

"You were saying?"

"I was saying that I didn't expect Ginger and Finks to pluck me up off the street right outside the door of Theobald Tramontina's apartment house, but it didn't knock me down either."

"Why is that?"

"Because when I was talking to Mrs. Tramontina, Theobald's aunt, and his niece, Ms. Shira Cardello, the young lady kept jumping up and going into the bedroom every couple of minutes. I don't have to be a genius to figure out what she was doing."

"Which was?"

"Calling you up for advice."

"What made you think that?" he asks, smiling at me sweetly.

"Because when I left, I figured she'd call up whoever she'd been calling again so she could give that person a final report. So I went to a pay phone and called the private number you give me the other day over to Delvin's and the number was busy."

"That's not proof."

"It made it a bet. So, now can I ask you a couple of questions?"

He takes a sip of water and waves his other hand at me, giving me permission.

"First of all, why did you decide not to ask me what you was going to ask me when we all met over to Delvin's house?"

He puts the glass down on the desk blotter.

"I informed Chips of my intentions. I told him I was going to send my people into his ward—your ward—in search of a missing relative."

"Tramontina?"

He nods his head. "A grandnephew by marriage, once removed."

"I don't understand these connections," I says. "I got cousins—two, three times removed—cousins I never even met calling me up asking for favors."

He sighs as though he agrees with me what a complicated mess family trees can be. Also what heavy obligations can be laid on a person because of some distant blood connection. "With Italians such relationships are very important. To use the bonds of family are the most important thing. Even more important than personal friendships."

"I understand. Why were you going to send people out searching for him?"

"Because Nonna asked me to look. He'd been missing for a month, more or less, and . . . you understand about Theobald?"

"Everybody tells me he wasn't very capable."

"You have the delicacy of a diplomat, Jimmy. That's a nice way of saying it. Theobald wasn't capable. He could do many things, you understand. He was not altogether disfunctional. The things he had most difficulty with, he learned to hide. He could fool you that he was nothing but a good-natured man who didn't take life too seriously."

"Is the only reason you was looking for him and the place he was staying in because Nonna asked?"

"An old woman, very close to death, was grieving for her missing child, afraid of what would happen to him if she died while he was away from home. Isn't that a good enough reason?"

"Sure. But someplace along the line, you found him and you stopped looking for him."

"What makes you say that?"

"First, Pescaro tells me to send my people out looking for Tramontina, then he tells me to forget about it."

"Well, after I had my people check the hospitals and the morgue—this name they gave him, Mr. Porky, delayed discovery—and my relative was found, there was no reason to have anybody go on looking."

"But you went on looking for his flat."

"Yes, we did, and when I told Delvin what we were doing and asked should I ask your permission, he said that he'd had word that you were interested in the matter. All I had to do, he said, was keep an eye on you and save myself a lot of running around."

"Okay, so what I'd like to know is what you expected to find."

"Who knows," he says.

He leans forward, folding his hands in front of him on the desk. "Theobald was slow, but he was still a man. You understand? He had appetites. It appears he met a woman. A girl much too young for him. Not too smart, but ambitious. A cheap woman who could be very expensive, yes? I'm told she had a way about her. He spent money on her. A lot of money he took from Nonna. But that's what foolish men who've got all their brains do around young women. That's not a major sin. Nonna asked me to inform the girl of Theobald's problem, to convince her it was not appropriate that she should have a relationship with a simple-minded man."

"Did Theobald know you interfered?"

"As it turned out, I wasn't the one to talk to her. Nonna also aired her troubles and concerns to other members of the family. Other branches. Who are not as subtle or as diplomatic as you and I."

"They leaned on her?"

"Enough to make her angry. Oh, she said she'd have no more to do with Theobald but, for spite, she told him why."

"And that's when he ran away," I says.

Vellitri leans back and takes another sip from his glass. He puts the expression of a saint on his face and says, "He ran too far—God grant him peace."

I'm living in a world full of actors.

"So that's the end of it," he says.

"I don't know that's the end of it," I says.

"Oh, yes, that's the end of it, Jimmy. You'll do me the favor."

So, there it was, right on the line. I've been going along for years doing favors for people and getting favors done back to me. So there always comes a time when somebody asks you for something it's hard for you to give— what goes against the things you believe in—but if you don't give it, you lose a relationship and you can never get it back. It's a very hard decision to have to make.

30

I ALMOST DO VELLITRI THE FAVOR AND LET IT go at that but the medicine bottle's in my pocket and a man's dead and nobody's told me anything to put my suspicions to sleep.

So I go over to the morgue to see Hackman again.

He's cutting somebody up as usual, but he stops what he's doing when he sees me walk in, peels off his gloves, and says, "Coffee break."

I follow him into his office.

He pours hisself and me a couple of cups of coffee. He lights hisself a cigarette—which he should know better, being a doctor—and then he leans back in his chair and looks at me for a long minute.

"All right," he says, "what I'm going to tell you now is not for publication."

"I ain't a member of the fourth estate," I says, making a little joke which he don't even bother smiling at.

"You've also got to promise me you won't even use it to stir things up unduly in your hunt for the truth about what happened to Mr. Porky."

"Theobald Tramontina," I says.

"That's right, he's got a name now, hasn't he? Maybe that's what decided me to share what I've found out with you."

"You've got my word," I says, making no more wise-cracks, "I won't just throw anything you tell me around, but I can't promise not to use it if I find out the truth's not so nice."

"That's all I want to hear, Flannery. One thing I know about you, you might bend the rules, steal a base, or come in through a back window if you can't get what you're after any other way, but I'd bet my life that you'd never break a promise or your word if you could help it."

I know I'm getting red from all that praise, but coming from a man like Hackman that kind of trust can mean a lot to a person.

"Mr. Tramontina died of a heart attack induced by the intromission of a toxin," he says.

"He was poisoned? Intromission's a funny way of putting it, ain't it?" I says.

He looks at me. His eyes are very piercing. "You've got a lot more language than people think you have, don't you, Flannery? You've got an ear for the exact meaning of words."

"Somebody said that a man with bad grammar wasn't necessarily stupid, but a man without vocabulary couldn't appreciate anything subtler than a smack in the kisser."

"Just so," Hackman says. "I say intromission because I'm not quite satisfied as to the method used to introduce the fatal dose. Was it by ingestion, injection, absorption, or respiration?"

"But you're still saying the man what dropped dead in front of my very eyes was poisoned?"

"That may very well be the case."

"Murdered?"

"I won't go that far. In fact it's not up to me to specu-
late about how the drug got into the body—by misadventure, oversight, or murderous intent."

"Drug?"

"The substance acts like a beneficial drug for certain
heart conditions and acts like a toxin to others not suf-
fering the disease. Now you understand why I don't
want you to use this information to push anything or
anybody?"

"I won't rock any boats don't need rocking," I says,
"and I won't quote you."

He gives me another one of his careful looks.

"You don't seem much surprised."

I hand him the bottle.

Hackman reads the label.

"That's the stuff," he says. "Where did you get this?"

"Somebody tossed it out in the garbage in the flat
where Tramontina was living. I just found it."

"But you suspected something the last time you came
to see me. Why was that?"

"I hear about how sometimes somebody's sitting having dinner at home or in a restaurant and they say,
'Please pass the grated cheese,' and before they have
time to sprinkle any on their pasta, they fall into their
plate face first. Dead as doornails. But here's a man on
his feet exercising and then he's on his back and the
next thing you know he's dead without a murmur or a
twitch. Also, when I take a look into his eyes, I see this
funny milky ring around the iris. I don't know what
that means. It could be cataract. What do I know? But
it shines in a very funny way—"

"Phosphorescence."

"—and that don't seem exactly right to me."

"Well, you caught something there, all right. The man
wore contact lenses and it may be that some of the

toxin gathered there in the tears around the lenses. Or it could be the means by which the toxin was introduced."

"Somebody put poison in his eyes?"

"It's very possible. This drug can be absorbed through the skin and membranes of the body."

Hackman stubs out his cigarette in the tin ashtray.

"Anything else you'd like to know, Flannery?" he asks, obviously ready to go back to work.

"No, I guess that's all. Except for one other thing."

"What's that?"

"What kind of contact lenses was Tramontina wearing?"

"He was near-sighted and astigmatic." There's a little smile on his face and he's giving me the old one-eye.

"I mean was he wearing the type you put in once and leave for a couple of days or a week? Or was he wearing the kind you got to clean with some kind of solution every now and then?"

"He was wearing hard lenses. Got to be cleaned daily," he says. "Okay?"

"Anything else I should know about them contacts?" I asks.

"Interesting point."

"What's that?"

"The contacts were tinted to change the color of his eyes. His eyes were brown but the lenses were blue. That tell you anything?"

"Just that somebody was playing games and got Mr. Tramontina to play games with them."

31

FATHER ROCCO ACTS LIKE HE'S GLAD TO SEE me when I show up on the doorstep of the rectory again.

"I don't want to take up any more of your time, Father," I says, "but there's something I—"

Before I can even get it all out, he's dragging me in by the sleeve.

"Who comes to ask my advice anymore? Who seeks my counsel? Who even wan's to siddown, tell a couple lies wit' an old man? Nobody, is who."

Over his shoulder I can see Angelina, his housekeeper, making a beeline down the hall from the back where she was probably in the kitchen, trying to beat the old priest to the door when the bell rang and mad because she didn't make it.

He turns around, pulling me in beside him and says, "Angelina."

"It's time for your nap. No interruptions," she says.

"Show a li'l charity, Angelina. Show a li'l Christian hospitality. Maybe you'll make my friend and me a coffee, maybe bring a dish of cannolis."

She raises her eyes to heaven the way women do when the men in their care insist on doing what they want to do, showing me that she ain't mad at me, she's just annoyed with the old priest.

She turns away and goes on back down the hall. Father Rocco looks up at me and grins in my face like we've put one over on the enemy.

"Father Harry's out on a mission of mercy, so at leas' we don' got him to worry abou'."

He shows me back into the old-fashioned library and we sit down like we sat before, in the worn leather chairs with an oak coffee table between us.

He folds his hands on his little belly and says, "How can I help you, my son?" almost like he done before.

I take out the piece of paper on which I made the mark with the potato stamp and hand it to him just as Angelina comes into the room with a tray on which is a silver coffee set, two cups and saucers, and a dish of Italian pastries.

She lays it down on the table and sees the piece of paper in Father Rocco's hand. She gives a gasp and makes the sign of the cross.

"Wha' are you doing?" Father Rocco asks. "There's nothing to be afraid of. It's just the same old nonsense."

"It's very bad," she says.

"Well, nobody sent it to me, so you can run along and stop thinking about it."

"You know that mark?" I says.

"Shoo. It's the Black Hand. You hear of this?"

"The Black Hand? I think it has something to do with the Mafia."

"What'd I teach you the other day? All the crooked Italians ain't necessarily Mafia. You unnerstan'? There's other thieves and bullies besides the Mafia."

"So is this *Camòrra* or *Unione Siciliana*?"

"None of them. The Black Hand isn' an organization—

a mob—it's a way of doing business. It's a way of extorting money. It was very popular with hoodlums back at the turn of century, the twennies. The poor ignorant immigrants come to this country, they think they not only got a chance for a better life but tha' they got away from the thieves and extortionists in the old country."

"But they came right on along," I says.

"Yes, the devil follows us wherever we go. They continued their threats. They terrorized the people. Sometimes they even killed people who wouldn' pay."

He's quiet for a minute, thinking back on them days.

Then he rouses hisself and says, "Go ahead, have some pastry. Don' insult Angelina. She's very sensitive."

"I'm supposed to be losing weight," I says.

"You don' wanna hurt her feelings. Eat. Eat."

I take a bite of one of the pastries and it's like I bit into a cloud. "Oh, God," I says.

"I'm sure He'd enjoy a piece of Angelina's pastry," Father Rocco says. "So this . . . what do you call it?—shakedown racket—it could be starting up again?"

"I don't know about that," I says. "I don't even know how this Black Hand business works."

"An Italian gets a threat, maybe a blackmail letter, from the Black Hand. They live in fear of a vague but terrible fate. They don' know who will be the victim—the father, one of the children, a relative, even all of them in a bombing, a fire, something like that."

"What's in the letter?"

"Usually a request for money, the place where it's to be delivered and, of course, the threat, the terrible consequences of a failure to comply. When the victim arrives at the designated place, there's no one there."

"In case the victim wasn't so scared and they called for help," I says, jumping ahead of him.

Father Rocco shakes his head and smiles wryly. He holds up a hand, telling me to listen and learn.

"He receives a second letter and after that, another and another and another until the victim is so *intimidi.* Heh?"

"Intimidated."

"Yes, exactly. The fear occupies the mind. He reads the letters over and over again. There are hints there. Hints about forgiveness for the imagined sins committed against the writer of the letters. Hints abou' approaching a 'frien'.' You unnerstan'?"

"Sure. The man's not paying off a blackmailer anymore, he's asking a person of some influence with the guy what's tormenting him to act as a go-between."

"No money has changed hands yet. Nobody has been paid off. This frien' is consulted. He's been standing by, solicitous and compassionate. If it is a new acquaintance, this new frien' has been very, very frien'ly. So he does the favor, this 'frien',' this go-between."

"And that's when the payoff finally gets made."

"Shoo. Because the 'frien' ' and the extortionist are the same person or are in league."

"Do they ever act out the threats?"

"Strong men have been known to resist without consequence. Often, in the past, there were beatings and murders."

We sit there, drinking coffee and munching on pastries.

"Does this piece of paper with the mark of the Black Hand on it have anything to do with Theobald Tramontina's death?" Father Rocco asks.

"You know about that?"

He looks at me with the sadness and patience of a very old man. "I was called out to give the last rites to Feliciana Tramontina. I may never be asked to do so again—there are younger men for such duties—but she asked for me in particular and I was honored to go. She died this morning."

"God bless her soul," I says. "I'm very sorry to hear that."

"No need for sorrow. She lived a pious life, a life of self-sacrifice. I always believed, were it not necessary that she take on the responsibility of her sister's child, she would've been a nun. Now she is in heaven with Jesus Christ, our Lord."

"Amen. Can you tell me the funeral home where they'll have the viewing? I'd like to pay my respects."

"She's been laid out at home. You hardly ever hear of that anymore. It's a very old-fashioned, old-country thing to do, but then, she was very old and very old-fashioned."

He smiles sweetly at me.

"Would you like some more cakes?" he asks.

I realize that I've finished off the whole plate.

Father Rocco laughs at the expression on my face.

"I better be going," I says.

He gets to his feet and walks with me all the way out to the front door.

"You never answered me," he says. "Was somebody threatening the poor simpleton with the Black Hand?"

"I found it at the place where he was living, Father. It looked like he could've been writing the notes."

Father Rocco frowns. "I can't believe a man with a flawed mind like Theobald's would think of such a thing."

"Neither do I, Father," I says.

32

I TAKE A CHANCE AND GO OVER TO THE CLUB
Morocco in Calumet City. It's early and it's the middle
of the week and there's not a lot of action in the club.
The guy on the door ain't even in uniform and he's
more bored than he was the last time I saw him.

"It's the alderman," he says. "How're things in the
Twenty-first?"

I don't correct him. I let it go. I figure it's easier.

"You must've found something you liked," he says.

"No, I didn't. That's why I thought I'd try again. I
heard about a beautiful dark-haired girl here by the
name of Marilyn LaFrance."

"Oh, sure, Mildred."

"Who?"

"Mildred Gallasi's her real name. Once she was Busty
Brown and once she was Sherry Flip and now she's Mar-
ilyn LaFrance but her real name's Mildred Gallasi. She's
Italian."

"I figured."

"A nice girl."

"That's what everybody says. That's why I'd like to meet her."

"So, you're in luck."

"How's that?"

"She was away for a couple of days, then she come back. Then she went away and now she's back again. These girls is like that. They're impetuous and undependable."

"So I better get inside before she decides to whip out the back door."

"Good idea."

He holds the door for me and I go inside. I don't see the hostess who clones Marilyn LaFrance on the spot. A waitress comes up to me and asks me do I want to sit at the bar because table and booth service won't start for fifteen minutes.

I say, sure, and she leads me over to the bar like I couldn't find it without her help. She takes my order for a ginger ale and walks it down to the service end where the bartender's talking to a cluster of girls. One of them in a powder blue outfit—a pair of tight, knee-length pants and a blouse that sticks out over her bare belly like a little tent—has dark hair cut in what used to be called a page boy.

When the waitress comes back to collect her five for the service, I ask her if the lady in the blue outfit is Marilyn LaFrance and she says she is, do I want to buy her a drink.

"If it's okay with her."

"Oh, it's okay with her," the waitress says.

"Make it a glass, not a bottle, of whatever she's having," I says. "I ain't staying long."

I watch the waitress deliver the message and order the drink. Then I watch as Marilyn or Mildred or whatever her name is walks toward me. I'm expecting a lot of hip wiggles and stuff like that, but she just walks one foot after the other like she's going somewhere. She's got a sweet face even when she gets closer and I can see all the makeup she's got on covering most of it up.

She slides onto the stool next to me and says, "Getting an early start?"

"Well, I thought maybe we wouldn't stay long."

The waitress sets Marilyn's drink down on the bar and collects another five from me.

" 'We,' is it, Red?" Marilyn says. "We married? We going steady? Because if we are, I ain't heard about it."

"Well, I could see the minute I walked into this place that it's going to be a slow night."

"So you want to make an early date?"

"How does that sound to you?"

"It sounds to me like somebody's been pulling your leg."

"What do you mean?"

"The girls in this place don't take dates and we don't turn tricks."

I can tell. She thinks I'm a cop and she's telling me she's a nun.

"You know me from somewhere?" I says.

"I never saw you in my life."

"Oh, I thought maybe you knew me and I done something to you sometime. Sometime I can't remember. Otherwise, why would you be acting so unfriendly?"

"You were described to me."

"I ain't a cop."

"I don't care you're a cop, you're not a cop. I'm not going anywhere with you."

There's a little perspiration on her upper lip and I can see she's scared. She thinks I want to get her alone outside so I can do her some harm.

"I'm not a cop and I'm not anyone sent to look for you by Teddy Tramontina or anybody connected to Teddy Tramontina. You know he's dead?"

"Oh, my God," she says, and I can see she's really distressed. "What happened?"

"It could be somebody stopped his heart."

As soon as I said it, I realized that could be taken two ways. I just meant that somebody gave him something that stopped it, but when she turns her head away, I see she thinks I mean it the other way, like somebody he loved busted it.

"I mean really stopped his heart," I says. "Not because his girlfriend left him."

"I wasn't his girlfriend. He might've thought I was, me letting him spend money on me. But that's what I do for a living," she says in this pleading voice like she's asking me to understand that there wasn't any harm meant just because she was trying to make a living.

"I understand what you're saying," I says.

"He was just a sweet, dumb, fat man. I used to tease him about it. I used to tease him that I was waiting for somebody with blue eyes and blond hair, about thirty years old."

"Teasing him?"

"Well, all right, I was telling him that I wasn't interested in anything like that with him. You know what I mean? I mean he was sweet but there was something about him you couldn't take serious. I wanted to let him down easy."

"You mean saying you wanted a boyfriend with blue eyes and all that?"

"That's right," she says, looking at me with these big eyes she's got. I look into them and I can see she probably ain't a helluvalot smarter than Theobald was.

"After his sister or his wife or whoever she was come flying in here and dragged him out, I told him that I didn't want to see him any more," she says. "I even took some sick days just so I wouldn't be here when he came in. Do you know he even came looking for me at this publishing house I done some work for? Some art photos?" Her voice went up at the end like she was making the last remarks questions.

"Some woman came in and dragged him out of here one time?"

"And told me to leave off. I tried to tell her I wasn't trying anything on, but she was out of here with him before I got a chance. Good-looking she was. Very classy. But you know what?"

"What?"

"I thought she was too hard for Teddy."

33

WHEN I GO TO THE FLAT ON A HUNDRED AND fifth and Avenue F, I can hardly find a place to park. There's big black limousines and fancy sports cars and four wheelers and all kinds of automobiles and pickups all up and down the street.

There's all kinds of people, all dressed up, the women in black dresses, the men with black bands on their sleeves. Kids're running up and down the block with mothers yelling at them to stay clean. There's such a crowd on the short flight of stairs leading to the porch and on the porch itself that I can hardly get through. But the people make way for a newcomer. They see the red hair and the Irish kisser and they treat the stranger coming to honor the old woman—who, even though she never had a kid of her own, was like the grandmother of this huge extended family—with respect.

In the hallway somebody's pulled out a table so people can pile their coats on it.

I step into the living room, which is a pretty good-sized room, the way they used to be in these old flats before we got better off and found out we had to live in a lot less because land and labor for building apartments and houses wasn't cheap anymore. The old lady's in her coffin set on a homemade bier in the window bay.

There's lot of women in black, all ages, and a lot of men, mostly on in years, except for this one group standing there in their twelve hundred dollar suits and two hundred dollar sunglasses.

Also I see Ginger and Finks sitting in folding chairs on either side of Vito Vellitri, who's got a place of honor down front.

I go up to the coffin and kneel down on the prayer stool and say a prayer for the old woman. When I get up and turn around, Vellitri's on his feet, looking at me, and Ginger and Finks is standing there, too. I walk up to him and say how sorry I am.

"Is that why you came, Jimmy, or is there another reason?"

"I'd like to talk," I says, glancing around, telling him we're too public.

"So, come with me," he says. Ginger and Finks start to fall in behind, but Vellitri says, "No, no. There's no need for you to come. Make yourself useful. See if Shira needs you for anything."

I follow him down the hall toward the bedroom. Before we go inside the room, I can see Shira at the kitchen table with some other women putting out cold cuts and salads. She looks up and sees me. I nod my head, telling her I'm there to pay my respects. Then she glances at Vellitri and goes back to what she's doing.

Inside the bedroom, Vellitri sits down on the satin bedspread. It's just like the one my mother—God rest her soul—used to be so proud of. There's a Sacred Heart of Jesus with some palm woven into a cross on top of it on one wall and a picture of the Madonna and Child on another.

Vellitri motions toward the stool in front of the dressing table and I sit down.

"I can't prove it, Vito," I says, getting right to it, "but I got every reason to believe that Theobald Tramontina was murdered."

He stares at me, then slowly blinks his eyes and nods his head.

"You know?" I says.

"Yes."

"You going to let it go at that?"

He puts his hand into the breast pocket of his jacket and takes out the photographs—or ones just like them—which we took from P. Pig's locker.

"Are they the photographs that—" I start to say.

"The same ones," he says. "The police have no more use for them. Or these."

He reaches into his side pocket and takes out four silver coins, Italian lire.

"You see this man, this well-dressed man with his dogs?" Vellitri says. "This man was Salvatore Tramontina, the grandfather. Not my grandfather, you understand. I came into the family through marriage but he was the *si masto*. You would say sir master."

"The head of the family," I says.

"More like chief," Vellitri says. "And this woman? This is Feliciana Tramontina, the sister who never married. The sister who cared for everyone after Salvatore was gone. That woman lying in her coffin in there."

He holds up his hand with the four coins in it and says, "There are five lire missing."

I take the silver coin out of my pocket and add it to the others in his hand.

"Do you know what these are?"

"Lire. Thirty lire. Thirty pieces of silver."

"You're Irish and you're Catholic, so you know the significance of thirty pieces of silver."

"That's what Judas got paid for betraying Christ."

"These were given to Theobald by Salvatore Tramontina when Theobald made his confirmation. It's a custom brought from southern Italy. It's to remind the young man never to betray. Never to betray Jesus Christ, his family, or a loved one. Theobald carried the pictures and the coins with him everywhere. They were his pride. They were a comfort to him."

I thought of him walking around in the wee hours of the morning, keeping the Amicos awake. I thought of Theobald up there in the practically empty flat night after night. I thought how the pictures and the lire hadn't been much comfort to him.

"You know why he left home, don't you, Vito?" I says. "You know about the Black Hand letters?"

"I know that there have been extortion attempts."

"You know who wrote the letters?"

"I have an idea."

"You know who played the go-between?"

He raises his eyebrows, surprised that I know about the way the extortion was played out.

"I'll find out, sooner or later."

"Then you don't have an idea yet who killed Theobald?"

He makes a gesture toward the door, the flat, the living room, the dead woman laying in her coffin.

"When I told you it was the end to it, I meant it was the end. I don't know what made Theobald run away from home and do such foolish things. That girl he said was his girlfriend? Maybe he wanted money to spend on her. Perhaps that was the reason. It was such a dangerous thing to do. A man like him. But Nonna grieved for him. She feared for what might happen to him after she was called to God. What she did was perhaps a bad thing to do but she meant it as an act of mercy."

"What are you talking about?"

"The woman who raised the orphan wanted him with her."

I finally get it. It's like we're talking about two different people but I don't know it until just now.

"You trying to tell me the old woman killed the person she cared for and protected since he was a kid?"

"I'm sure she thought there was no other way to protect him except to take him with her."

"How'd she get the heart medicine into him?"

"Theobald had called her in the night. He was lonely and told her where he was staying. She took a taxicab and went to see him. His eyes were red from the contact lenses he wore. She gave him a bottle of eye drops."

"How'd she know it would kill him?"

"Her doctor had warned her to be very careful with the drug. He wanted her not to keep it in the medicine cabinet with other things for fear someone would mistake them for nose drops or eye drops and have a fatal accident."

"She tell anybody else about this?"

"Only me."

Maybe it's the best story he can come up with on the spur of the moment, but it's pretty bad.

"That's a story I wouldn't want to have to sell to a cop," I says.

"I already sold it to a cop," he says. "Have you got a different story?"

"I think in a big family like your wife's family that comes from the old country and scatters across a city, some of them end up being rich—one way or another— some of them do all right, and some of them end up being the poor relatives. I got a feeling that the Cardellos ended up that way. Not starving but still the poor relatives."

He gives me half a nod, which coming from Vellitri is a big yes.

I tell him how I think Shira got the idea to make some fast money, some big money. The whole trick with the Black Hand was that the extortionist never came right out and exposed hisself. The payoff was put into a 'friend's' hand. Shira used poor Theobald for a cat's paw. She played on his vanity. She got him to play the game and write the letters in case somebody came looking for the blackmailer with blood in their eye. No matter what happened, she was just a young woman doing a favor for a relative, delivering a message and accepting an envelope that could've been the return of a loan for all she knew.

"She's got a sense of humor, Shira has. She's got a sense of the ironical and she wanted a little get-back from the rich relatives," I says. "So she went after some of them and they didn't let it rest. They were connected and people went looking. So she decided to shut down the operation."

Another half a nod and a blink.

"Theobald got the drug into him by using eye drops," I says. "It was Shira gave them to him. She was shutting down the operation and she decided to shut Theobald down, too, just to be on the safe side."

"You got proof of what you say?" Vellitri asks, and I know right there he's been looking for Theobald's killer. And he's been looking around for the Black Hand extortionist, too, which was why Shira closed it down.

"Marilyn LaFrance told me about the night when Shira came looking for Theobald down at the Club Morocco, but when I told her and Nonna about me finding the flat he was staying in, she acted like it was news to her."

Vellitri stands up.

There's a knock on the door.

"What is it?" Vellitri asks.

The door opens and Shira comes halfway in.

"Some of the family's leaving and want to say good-bye to you," she says.

"This is family business, Mr. Flannery," Vellitri says, being very formal with Shira in the room. "I'll take care of it."

"I don't know if I can let you do that, Mr. Vellitri," I says.

Shira's looking at first one of us and then the other. She's got a good idea of what we're talking about. I can tell she's afraid.

"I know what kind of man you are," Vellitri says. "You're a man who knows how to cut a corner and bend a rule. You understand that there's the law and then there's justice. You've even taken it into your own hands now and then. Do I have to remind you?"

"But I ain't never executed anybody."

"Neither will I, Mr. Flannery," Vellitri says. "Neither will I."

He walks over to Shira and puts his hand on her shoulder. "Let's go say good-bye to the family," he says. She closes her eyes. All the color's gone from her face. Her lipstick looks like a smear of blood on her mouth. She goes down the hall with her cousin by marriage, once removed.

I have an idea what's going to happen to her. She'll live. They'll find her a place in one of their homes where she'll play the part of the maiden aunt, a servant to those she tried to do an injury. She won't be wearing those tailored slacks and high heels anymore. The children will call her aunt and she'll never marry because if she'd known how to live separated from the family in the first place, she'd never have had to do what she thought she had to do in order to get what she thought she had coming to her. If she asked, maybe they'd let her become a nun, but that wasn't done as much as it used to be anymore.

Then again, maybe not. Maybe she'll go to another city and make herself a life. Maybe she'll turn out to be the CEO of some big company. Maybe she'll show up on television. Who knows? These are different times.

When I stop down to the police station and share these thoughts with Pescaro, he shrugs and says, "Hey, Flannery, you and me both know there's a lot of killers walking the streets. Some of them never get caught. Some get caught and never come to trial. Some come to trial and then walk out free people after a jury acquits them for lack of evidence or the evidence is declared fruit of a poisoned tree or whatever. I don't know if there's a heaven or a hell where things get evened up, but I think if somebody kills another person like Shira Cardello killed Theobald Tramontina—if that's what really happened—they're going to be punished sooner or later, one way or another."

He must've read the doubt on my face. Here's a funny one, I think, the skeptical, hardened, bitter cop trying to tell the everything's-coming-up-roses, cock-eyed optimist that things work out for the best, one way or another.

"Then again, maybe not," Pescaro goes on. "Either way, it ain't up to me or you. We did what we could for Tramontina. Now somebody else's going to have to take it the rest of the way because there's nothing else you and me can do.

"The way it happens sometimes, Jimmy," Pescaro says. "An ambitious person like this woman gets away with it once, she tries it again and the next time she don't get away with it. The next time we nail her."

That don't make me feel any better. It just makes me sad to think that the only thing we come up with after all these thousands of years of struggling with crime is that sooner or later we can *maybe* get the chance to hurt somebody who hurt somebody else. An eye for an eye and a tooth for a tooth ain't the most satisfying windup in the world.

So I go home and trudge up the six flights of stairs to my flat, feeling like I'm only a year or two younger than the old lady in her coffin. When I open the door, Alfie comes running up to greet me. I hear voices and laughter from the living room.

Mary, my old man, Aunt Sada, and Mary's mother Charlotte, are sitting in there having a good time.

"That ain't champagne you're drinking, is it, Mary?" I says before I even say hello.

"Just a sip in celebration," she says.

"Celebration of what?" I says.

"The engagement of my mother and your father," she says. Everybody starts laughing at the expression on my face.

Later on when they've gone home, I tell Mary I always thought that if my father decided to get married again, it'd be to Aunt Sada.

"I mean they was always joking and fighting with each other. Your mother just sat there, quiet as a mouse, taking it all in."

"Your mother was a quiet woman, too," Mary says. "Mike told me about her."

"That's right, she was," I says. "God bless her."

34

So MARY AND ME ARE BACK ON THE ROUTINE, which most people would call a mess.

Mondays, I'm at the storefront listening to complaints and requests, doing what I can do for the people in the Twenty-seventh. Mary's in the other office seeing pregnant girls and women.

Tuesdays, I'm over at the Paradise doing the leg lifts.

Wednesdays, Mary's at the clinic over to Mary Thompson Hospital.

Thursdays, I'm huffing and puffing again.

Fridays, Mary's over to the clinic again.

Saturday afternoons, I'm at Brennan's talking to my precinct captains. Evenings, I'm at the Paradise again, punishing myself.

Which gives Mary and me Sundays together, during most of which the phone's ringing off the hook with people needing this or that.

Mary's getting bigger and bigger.

I'm getting skinnier but it makes me feel weak and I'm hungry all the time.

A few weeks go by. I'm thinking about how I'm starting to feel like a burnt-out match. I'm thinking about
giving half of it up, quitting the party organization, quitting the exercise classes, quitting all the running around
and doing for people. I'm thinking about putting my feet
up and just getting fat.

"What are you brooding about, James?" Mary asks one
Sunday afternoon.

I unload all my gripes on her.

"I think you're absolutely right," she says.

"How's that?" I says, very much surprised because I
was expecting an argument or at least a little friendly
persuasion.

"It's crazy for us to eat ourselves up the way we do.
When all's said and done, how much do we really
accomplish?"

"Well . . ." I says.

"I mean we've got government agencies that are supposed to take care of these problems and concerns."

"Well . . . " I says.

"We pay our taxes. We pay the salaries of policemen
and firemen and social workers and—"

"Well, I can tell you, Mary, there ain't enough of
them. There ain't enough of any city employees, no
matter what people might think. There just ain't
enough bodies to go around and take care of everything
that needs taking care of."

"Hire more people," she says.

"Well, it ain't only hiring more people. It's the enthu-
siasm you got to have. The dedication. Like nowadays
every time there's a budget crunch with the schools, they
take something nice away from the kids. Like music or
art classes. Like this or that. When I was a kid, the teach-
ers stayed after school—no pay—just to give the kids that
something extra, you know what I mean?"

"Can't expect people to work for nothing, James," she says.

"What about satisfaction? What about giving something back? What about . . ."

I stop right there. I know what she's doing to me. She's pulling Mike's old trick where he steals your arguments and turns them around on you.

"There are things that need doing and there aren't enough people doing them, James," she says, being very quiet. "If not us, then who? If not now, then when?"

"Maybe that's it," I says. "Maybe there's so much that needs doing and so few people doing it, that I can't see the end of the road. Like with these young women—these kids—coming to the storefront on Monday nights. They're children themselves and they're going to be having babies. So you get them through the deliveries okay—more or less okay—so what comes after? The simple basic things they ain't got and can't afford. I'm telling you, Mary, I can't see the end of the road."

"There isn't any end to it, James. You know that. We're not trying to get any particular place so we can stop doing and stop being. We're on the journey and ain't we lucky . . ."

I'm surprised, she hardly ever says "ain't" and used to correct me about it all the time until she gave up on my grammar.

". . . ain't we lucky we've got each other?" she says. "Most of these girls haven't got someone of their own like we've got."

"We got to do something for them," I says, feeling frustrated and helpless.

"So, think about it, James. We can't take care of the world. You're always saying that. We can't even take care of all the pregnant women in this ward. But we can make it better for at least a few. And that's all we should expect to do. So, you think about it, Jimmy. You always come up with something, an angle, a back door, a hole in the roof. It's your gift."

Ten days later, about five of the welfare mothers-to-be from Mary's storefront clinic are due to have their babies practically any minute.

Mary pulls a few strings here and there. I call in a few favors and trade a couple more, so that I get one of the seven members of the Medical Center Commission to throw her weight our way.

We get all five admitted to the maternity ward at River-edge Hospital.

I go over there.

Mary's rushing around in her nurse's smock, looking like a ship under sail—looking like she's ready to have her own baby any minute.

The nurses are all hyped up. The doctors are all hyped up.

"What's going on, Mary?" I asks.

"It's one of those things you read about," she says. "All five of our mothers delivered within five minutes of one another."

"That's something you could get on the news, maybe get a little attention," I says.

"It's already going to be on the news," she says. "Billy Behan was nosing around, following me like he's been doing. I saw him lurking in the corridors like some sort of character in a spy movie."

"I'll tell him to—" I start to say, getting a little hot under the collar.

"No, no," Mary says, obviously getting a big kick out of it. "It couldn't have worked out better. I got the idea of putting all the babies in the bed with each of the mothers in turn. Take pictures. You know? It was like they were all one big family? And who pops in to see what's going on but Billy Behan. He sees the five infants in the same bed with Mrs. Quintana's granddaughter Rosa, and he jumps to a conclusion."

"What's that?"

"You must be slowing down, James, if you don't see the angle. If you don't see what Billy Behan thought he was seeing."

I feel this grin starting up from my toes somewhere. "You mean Billy thought that Rosa'd had quintuplets?"

Mary's nodding at me, grinning as much as me.

"He went running out of here begging us not to call the newspapers. Not to call the TV stations. Begging us to just give him the chance to get a cameraman and get back here to get the story before we called anybody else," she says.

"Hey, Mary," I says, "nobody planted this idea in his head?"

"No, I swear. He jumped to the conclusion all by himself."

"We don't want to lie to anybody here," I says.

"I'd never do that, James. When he asks, I'll give him Rosa's name and that's all. While he runs off at the mouth the way he does, I'll just nod my head or shake my head accordingly."

"Because, I mean, we don't want to be accused of misleading or misinforming the press," I says.

"Leave it to me," Mary says. "I won't let Billy Behan shoot himself in the head, but if he insists on shooting himself in the foot, there's nothing I can do about that."

She holds out her arms and I give her a hug, which ain't easy what with her belly and my belly.

"You know what?" I says. "A couple of weeks ago you said I had a gift, that I always came up with something, an angle, a back door, a hole in the roof. Well, you know how they say that people who live together a long time start to talk like each other and look like each other and even start to think like each other?

Lately I notice you been saying 'ain't' every now and then." I look down at where our bellies are touching. "I'm hoping that after you have the baby and get skinny, I'll get skinny. And when it comes to thinking tricky like me, it looks like you're doing that, too."

Billy Behan comes rushing back with this free-lance photographer he knows, and they snap a lot of pictures of Rosa and the babies. When he goes hurrying past me out the door, I says, "Billy, you sure you want to go off half-cocked like this?"

"What do you mean, what do you mean?" he says. "I got this scoop and I ain't going to let anybody take it away from me."

For a second there I almost tell him that newspapermen don't talk about things like scoops anymore but, what the hell, he seems to be enjoying hisself—smiling with happiness for the first time since I can hardly remember when—so I don't.

"Maybe you learned something about me today, Flannery," Behan says. "I ain't just an investigative reporter, digging up cases of malfeasance, misfeasance, or nonfeasance. I'm always happy to report good news, too."

I almost grab him by the arm and tell him what's what, but he's out the door and running and I ain't in good enough condition to go running after him.

I go in to see all them little kids. They got their little faces all scrunched up and their tiny hands are making fists. A couple of them are crying, mad as hell that they been pushed out of their nice warm nests.

For God's sake, they're starting their travels and they don't even know it and they're mad as hell.

I feel like they're my kids. I feel like I'm the orchestra leader getting everybody to come in when they're supposed to come in. I know that I ain't got a thing to do with it, but still and all, that's the way I feel.

*   *   *

The story comes out, quintuplets born at River-edge.

Quintuplets ain't as unusual as they were once upon a time, what with these fertility drugs and everything, but on a slow news day they're worth a subhead and a minute on the morning news.

A half a dozen city officials come down to make a fuss, led by my old Chinaman, Delvin, and his chum, Dunleavy. My captains are there and the organization from the First.

The mayor and part of his staff show up. There's so much crime and strife they got to go to the people about, here's a chance for them to associate themselves with an event that warms everybody's heart.

The five little babies, like practically all little babies, look enough alike to be brothers and sisters. There's two boys and three girls.

Then the calls start coming in from the stores and wholesalers, from the small merchants and big manu-facturers. Offers of cases of formula, diapers, bottles, nipples, layettes, furniture, scholarships, free rent for a year.

Everybody's jumping aboard, eager for the opportunity to do a well-publicized good deed while reaping public relations awards.

Something for something.

Nothing wrong with that.

By the time the truth comes out—maybe a week later—everybody's still feeling so good that they say they can understand how a mistake could be made with everybody so busy, all that confusion, five babies being born within maybe five minutes of one another.

So nobody takes nothing back.

Billy Behan gets an offer of a job with a neighborhood weekly which wants him because they do easy-going neighborhood stuff which they never knew before that he was very good at.

And one Monday morning Mary gives me a poke and wakes me up.

"Jimmy," she says, "the baby's coming."

"You sure?" I says.

She grins and says, "I ain't been a nurse all these years for nothing."

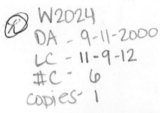

W2024
DA - 9-11-2000
LC - 11-9-12
#C - 6
copies 1

DISCARD

9-91

F   Campbell, Robert
        In a pig's eye